THE ROAD TO CHIDARRA

KEITH B. PERRIN

Dedicated to my friend, my Lord and my Master,
my true inspiration, The Lord Jesus Christ.

I would like to acknowledge:

Nika Wong for front and back book cover art:
Nika_wong@yahoo.com

Omaik for interior sketches, Omaik@hotmail.com

Griffen Engel: dragon of Laurogor. sketch,
griffinjengel@gmail.com

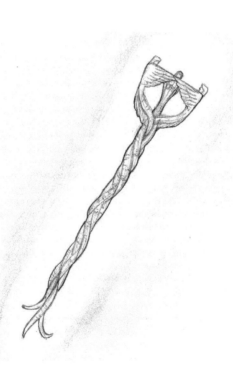

ONE

JOURNEY THROUGH ARGONIA

The night was quiet and dark on the lonely, craggy, rocked mountainside. A heavy mist and thick fog draped over the land as far as the eye could see. Even far down in the valley below the forest of Argonia, it was unusually silent.

The moon is bright and aglow but shadowed by the overcast of clouds that cloak its light. One could not see two feet in front of them with the conditions of this night. There are very few trails through Argonia and fewer still who traverse these parts. There is not a town or village for many leagues, and only a few mountain folk or woodsmen call this place home, those who are rugged and adept at dealing with the many dangers lurking there.

There was a rustling through the forest, a faint glow of light moving up a wooded path. A hooded, dark-cloaked figure, with his face covered, suddenly appeared out of the misty darkness. An old gray bag with items of some kind rested behind his back, held up by a strap upon his shoulder.

A long old wooden staff helped to guide him through the misty forest until a worn and barely legible sign appeared. It was carved in the bark of a large tree at a fork in the road and was written in a strange, unknown language. The cloaked figure looked on and began softly humming a song as the fog began to dissipate around him just enough to see a faint blue glow from an old stone marker on the ground to his left. Taking a deep breath, he began humming again. A strong wind blew, making a long dark but clear path off the trail and through dense overgrown brush keep lighted by more glowing stones spaced far apart on the ground. Holding his lantern in front of him, he walks on until he reaches a clearing, and he sees the side of a large mountainside illuminated by moon and starlight, with a long windy stone staircase carved out of the mount and speckled with glowing stones upon the steps to light one's way.

Taking a deep breath and putting the staff in his sash, he climbed the path until he reached a hidden crevice just large enough for a man to walk through.

The figure rested for a few seconds, picked up the lantern, and slowly walked through the dark and damp crevice. Strange markings and symbols were visible but faded on the floor and walls by the dulling light of the lantern. Deeper and deeper, he went in the mountain before coming to a room that the lantern barely illuminates. More dust and grime covered symbols, and writings are seen on the walls, with carvings of strange beasts and faces of men from long ago.

Putting the lantern up to the wall, the light reveals faded wall paintings of ancient kingdoms and battles that have now been forgotten, along with otherworldly creatures that would seem to be of one's fantasy or dreams, if not nightmare, as if to issue a warning for those who come across them. The figure wipes away dust and grime from the paintings with his hand to see a scratched, tarnished mural that showed a fierce giant battling a lone warrior and celestial beings dwelling among the stars.

The air became rank, and the figure decided to move on, looking for another path until he spied dust-covered stairs carved out of rock, spiraling upward. The lantern's flame began to flicker when he softly sang a hymn that echoed through the cavern. Suddenly ancient wall torches that used to light the way up and down the stairs in the days of old began to light up, thus paving the way for the cloaked figure to walk in light up and not darkness. Up he went until he reached the top, where the moonlight shone through the clouds and the mists began to recede. To the left was a small room carved out of the mountainside, with a small window and rotted wood shutters that thick spider webs covered.

A small round stone table with old wooden chairs and a stone bench carved out of the mountain rock sat idly while in the corner near the window was a small fireplace with a lump of wood ash still in its pit and two fire prongs that rested on each side of the fireplace. The stranger put the lantern that flickered on the table, along with the rest of his goods, and then pulled out a small dagger from his bag. Then he walked outside to three white-barked trees with low-hanging leafy branches.

Taking the dagger, he cut down enough branches to make a soft bed. He then went over to bushes around the rocks and cut sticks and brush from them to start a fire. Walking in the room, he put the old dry wood from the chairs and the brush from the bushes into the fireplace. Then he opened a small bag on his waist and grabbed flint and steel to try to start a fire, but that didn't work, so he went inside the stairwell and grabbed one of the old torches and used it to light the fire. He gave thanks, warming his hands and face. Then he took the soft, lush leaves, made a bed out of them on the cold, damp stone floor, and fell fast asleep.

Night became morning and morning night again until after three days of sound sleep, he slowly awakened to the smell of broiled fish and hot bread wrapped in a white cloth. A flagon of milk, wine, and water each sat with the food on the stone table. Suddenly out of the corner of his eye, he saw three large ravens looking at him in the window. They quickly flew away. The cloaked figure looked at the fireplace to see it still burning strong and then slowly stood up and yawned, looking at the rotted, cobwebbed shutters lying broken on the ground.

Looking out the window, he notices two large stone figures holding staffs and wearing crowns, with both hands raised to the heavens, their bearded faces looking upward, covered in vines and vegetation. Betwixt them was a large stone altar that he did not notice in the dark. Yawning again, he slowly uncovers his head and disrobes, revealing a tall, brown-skinned, well-built form, his long black braided locks, tied in twine, reaching the center of his back.

His eyes were sullen and fierce yet full of wisdom, compassion, and purpose. Lastly, his beard was trimmed short and black.

The man took the water and washed his hands and face, then turning, he bowed his head, giving thanks for the meal and ate. When his belly was full, he gave his attention to his staff, which was lying by his sack on the floor. He held it in his hands and closed his eyes as if to sense something. Then he turned around and walked outside and was greeted by the dawn of a new day. The ground was wet for it had rained for two nights, but he had slept through the storm, warm and dry, without any sense of it. His sullen eyes beholding the rising of the golden sun, he hears in the distance the sound of rushing water.

Leaving the shelter, he walks around the mountainside on a path lined withrocks and rough foliage. There he finds a small water-fall, where the trapped clear rainwater rushed down the mountain.

The man began to undress and wash himself. He was aged, but this belied the stout and rigid frame that was of a man much younger. Scars etched deep upon his back, arms, and chest tell of past battles. While bathing himself, he began to heave deeply, and leaning against the stones, tears began to fall. They were washed away by the flow-ing water. He let out a wail that echoed long throughout the valley below, shaking the rocks of the mountain.

After this, he picked himself up and encouraged himself with a silent prayer and began to sing and sing and sing so loudly that the psalm overcame the heaviness within him. Then he stepped out of the cool water flow and dried himself off with a rag from his bag. Reaching for his brown tunic and pants, he washed them and let them dry on the rocks from the heat of the sun. Then he walked back and pulled out a cloak that was scarlet with silver trim and donned it until his clothes dried.

Reaching back in his sack, he pulled out a pair of leather boots that seemed to have special meaning to him, like the scarlet cloak, and wore them.

After his clothes had dried, the stranger put them on and cov-ered his head with a long tasseled cloth. Kneeling down by the large rock altar, he spoke words deep within and would not look up.

Shaking and alone, the mysterious man started to utter deep groans, as if in travail or some distress.

Then in the warmth of the noonday, a cloud slowly came from the east against the wind. It overtook and surrounded him, and he began to see a vision. He saw lands, kingdoms, and peoples of various tribes toward the west, beyond these mountains and dark forests, bent on decay and driven to madness. The people seemed filled with terror and under cruel bondage. Then he hears a voice uttering dark sentences, but suddenly the vision stops. The cloud remains surrounding him so that half of the side of the mountain was hidden beneath it. Soft flashes of lightning without thunder flicker within the cloud as it darkens and becomes thicker in stark contrast to the blue skies and sunny day far above, illuminating the lands.

"Master," the stranger prays, "though strong in mind and body, I am worn beyond all measure in spirit. This journey has been long and hard, and I have not traveled here in many moons. The kingdom of Itvihiland and its outposts are long gone. Only Edeicia, this deserted temple of the mountain prophets of old, remains. And it brings deep sadness within me."

Then a voice responds, "That is not the only reason you feel sorrow. Go to the lands and peoples I will lead you to, for many of their cries reach my throne. Darkness has ruled these lands and the people there, but it is my wish to see them free and to know my name."

At this, the voice stopped and departed from his presence, along with the thick cloud, revealing the radiance of the sun.

Then the man walks over to the room and cleans it up, honoring those who once dwelled there. Looking around, he grabs his belongings and begins to walk down the long spiral stairwell. This was a dreary and lonely place, a long-forgotten relic of the past with dirt- and mire-covered steps. Large cobwebs and spiders move above, and he feels a strange wind pass by him. Eerie growls sound from below.

The old torches begin to weaken and flutter. The cloaked figure was reaching into his sack for the lantern when the torches flickered out. He grabs for his staff, and it begins to shine, changing into a glowing sword that hums a faint song. Its light blazes a path so he can see.

His heart beating fast, he stands deathly still. He points the sword down so he can spy the winding staircase below.

A snarling creature of darkness, dreadful and terrible to behold, lurched up from the depths. Its eyes are large and black, and it is hairless, with greenish pale skin. A foul odor reeks from the beast, and it begins to howl and wail aloud. It was bred to see in the darkness, and the teeth that protrude grotesquely from its mouth chatter together, foam and blood oozing out, awaiting the taste of human flesh.

Suddenly the man is grabbed from behind by another beast the same as the first, and a mighty struggle ensues. The creature from behind him opens its mouth to bite him, but his sack keeps it at bay, and he grabs it by the throat and throws it at the first, making both of them tumble down the stairwell. However, the beasts have the advantage, for darkness is their friend.

As he hurries down the stairs, the light of his sword shows the true nature of the danger about him, for this place is full of flesh-eating creatures desiring to tear him apart. High-pitched howls and shrieks are heard throughout the chamber now, and he realizes if he is to survive, he must act quickly. The warrior's sword begins to crackle, and lightning bursts forth, burning the ravenous hordes beneath him and hurling them back.

Then he turns it above him to disperse the creatures, who cry aloud in pain. Again, he points the sword downward to see the distance and runs swiftly to the ground, where the hunched-over beings await him on the walls, ceilings, and floor. As he lands, they surround him, awaiting to feed with clawed hands open.

He cries out, "Tempest sing!"

Then Tempest, the great battle sword, bane of evil and the crack of doom, sings a loud hum as it leaves his hands and begins to swirl around and around, reaching great speeds, cutting in twain many of the creatures, leaving bloody half corpses and burnt bodies in its wake. Those left are blinded by the light Tempest shines on them, and they scurry off, howling into the darkness.

All becomes silent and still. The smell is nauseating, but at that moment, it matters not to him. He is back where he began, at the entrance of the stairwell where the old paintings and ancient artifacts lay coated in dust. The light of Tempest makes it easy for him to see what he missed earlier—bones of men long dead, ripped and torn books laden with dust, dried blood, and cobwebs. Around the corner was the great temple hall where holy worship was offered, but he feared to enter to see the condition of it.

On each side were long hallways and rooms carved out of the mountain that the sword's light barely revealed, but it was the old iron doorway at the base of the winding stairs that caught his attention. Slowly and carefully, he opens the creaky door to find many ancient tools instruments of worship and weapons encased in crystal. They were special and not to be handled lightly, needing to be encased so as to not enter the wrong hands. The warrior lays his hand upon the crystal and silently utters a prayer when it dissolves. Hearing more wails, he realizes he must hurry and grabs a shield, bow, harp, cloak, an ax, and a flute.

He sees a gold-colored bag hanging on the wall, and he puts the items in it, but strangely, the bag felt light, as if holding very little. After leaving the room, the crystal reappears and encases it once again. The brown-skinned warrior drapes the bag behind him and slowly walks to the great hall. It is cold and dark, and the stink is strong. Cautiously he enters, tossing Tempest in to float and light the way so he can see clearly. Tempest hums once again, shining very brightly. He can see a room with large pillars laced with gold, ivory, and silver and beautiful art that have become worn stripped and broken down. Claw marks are etched deep upon the pillars walls and armor of ancient guardians. A large crater rests in the floor, with eerie wails sounding forth from it. Desecrated, chewed-upon skeletal remains are sprawled everywhere. Destroyed tables chairs and temple artifacts made of precious ores and jewels lay melted and burned. A desperate battle had raged here. Then the altar shone far in the front of the sanctuary with a replica of the great Ark of the Covenant. Overhead the sanctuary hung large black leathery sacks, dangling high in the ceiling and rafters. Evil reptiles and things unseemly slithered around, unfazed by his presence.

The place was charred with fire and ash, but he kept looking at the Ark.

"This shouldn't be," he said, fearing the state of the enigmatic Ark.

He walks over the bones of friend and foe alike as Tempest floats on ahead. It begins to shine brighter when he sees the true horror that has taken place. The black sacks are not sacks at all but immense, leathery bat-like creatures with dreadful red eyes, sharp fangs, and long thick barbed tails that begin to slowly stir and awaken. He then sees the Ark begin to move and shake and slowly open. A thick green smoke arose from it. Suddenly a tall, gaunt, powerful being from the nether realm that slept in the Ark to mock God and the memory of all that was once holy there took form. It was veiled in darkness and covered in smoke that hid its form from view. Only its shimmering yellow eyes could be seen through the smoke and the jewel-crested crown of flame and ash that rested upon its head.

Angered by what he saw, the warrior shouted, "Blasphemy!"

Then the hellish creature points its long, gangly, gnarled finger, speaking in a mocking whisper, "You are of the order of the ancient warrior prophets, are you not?"

The man says nothing as astonishment and rage grips his soul.

"You are the first to enter here since the ruin of this temple centuries ago. You should have seen the slaughter, the pain and agony on their faces when they called upon their deity for aid and none came. The looks of despair and cries of abandon were music to our ears. Oh, they put up a good fight, just not good enough, as you can see."

Then the creature floods the prophet's mind with images of what happened to those long dead—sights of blood and bones bathing the walls and floors throughout, burnings and tortures and the desecration of the holy temple and its sacred books and beautiful art, the large golden menorah that would no longer hold its light melted and spoiled. Not one soul was spared as legions of evil brought this place low.

The mountain shakes with loud heavy footsteps, and a roar of something large approaches from below, led by thick black smoke and dust spewing from the pit. The prophet backs slowly, saying nothing as Tempest hovers between him and the creature standing upon the altar next to the ark. Tempest points its blade at the monster and lets out a flash of light as if angered by its taunts. "At least your blade has courage enough. I'd depart while I could."

"Come to me, Tempest." He beckons, and the sword floats back in front of its master, leading him out of the great hall and finally out of the lonely cavern. He left the dark creature that was mocking, cursing, and laughing at him while the mountain shook with roars of rage from whatever approached from the depths. Saying nothing, he ties the golden sack up and carries it down the long narrow path of smooth steps with peppered glowing stones concealed by the light of the sun, Tempest floating by his side.

His heart heavy, tears flowing from his eyes from the words spoken by the creature that dwells in the great hall where it ought not to, he reaches the ground and in somber thought, looks back up at the windy stairs to the mountain entrance, grinding his teeth, anger upon his face. However, he knows he is needed elsewhere, and vengeance upon that foul creature and his minions must wait for another day so the gleaming blade transforms back into the wooden staff in the hand of the prophet. He looks at the rays of the sun shining through the leaves of the trees. Covering his head, he begins anew his journey back through the path from whence he came.

As soon as he reached the fork in the road where the ancient glowing marker had been, the path was again concealed by trees, thick underbrush, and thorns with thistles that quickly regrew, making it undetectable and once again forgotten by nigh all, veiled in the mists of time.

TWO

OF HAGS AND BONES

Days go by, and the hooded prophet, weary of heart, leaves the path and rests under the shade of an apple tree. After eating of its fruit, he begins to enter a deep slumber, only to be awakened by the sound of children playing and the singing of song. A dog barks while the sound of horse and carriage clump along the trail. His eyes open after dreaming of a shimmering white steed.

"Hello, why are you sitting there all alone?" asked two small olive-skinned children. Both had dark brown hair, lovely brown eyes, and a look of innocence that contrasts the perils around them.

He pulls back his hood to reveal his brown face and long locks.

"Hello," he says to the children, who are healthy but modestly dressed, both wearing talismans around their necks. Then he smiles and pets the dog that laps him in the face.

"Bruno likes you," said the little girl.

"What's in the golden sack?" asked the boy.

The prophet chuckles when their mother hurries over and grabs them from behind.

"Don't be afraid, fair maid. I am no threat," he says in her native language. "I am Feneer and have business to the west."

"Oh, and what might that be?" asks the woman suspiciously. "Argonia is not a place for strangers to be wandering about."

"Agreed," says Feneer, nodding his head.

"Are you a wizard or medicine man? If not, you sure look the part."

"Neither," he responds softly.

"Do you have lodging?" she asks.

"No, I do not, and if it wouldn't be much trouble to you, I would like to."

The children interrupt and beg their mother to let him stay as she looks him over keenly. She finds no ill feeling and bids him to come along. He thanks her for her kindness and generosity.

Feneer sits in the carriage next to the woman and rests his weary feet, looking at the grassy hillside and bright blue sky with little clouds above. Only a lush canopy of trees on the right of the path shields them from the heat of the sun.

The little red-haired dog, Bruno, barks the whole way until they reach an old wooden gate. The woman sitting on the carriage behind the horses bids the children to open the gate, and they enter a well-traveled dirt-and-rock pathway.

The prophet looks around and smells water, but he cannot find it until to his left, he sees a large pond hidden away by trees and tall brush. Next to the pond, he sees a stone cottage with smoke coming out of the chimney.

"This is your home, I presume?" says Feneer.

"You presume right," the woman responds with a smile on her face. "Come on, children. We're having roast duck and muffins for dinner."

The children run to an old two-level home with a wooden porch. Their small farm, with chickens, pigs, goats, and cows, rests quietly in this remote area. Feneer takes a deep breath and jumps off the carriage, chasing the children around the yard, making sport. After dinner, Miriam formerly introduces herself and her two children, Anna and Cory, to the prophet. They tell him how their father went missing over a year ago. The prophet notices the many idols present in their abode.

Sorrow shrouds Miriam after mentioning the loss of her husband, but she takes a deep breath, holding on to her children. Later, Feneer was shown his washing and sleeping quarters in the small guest room. It was warm and cozy, with a soft bed and small icons in the windowsills to ward off evil spirits.

Cory knocked on his door again, asking what was in the golden sack, but the prophet said nothing, shutting the door. His heart felt heavy for these kind people who have endured such a loss. His inner spirit was grieved for something, but he could not tell what it was, so he prayed and asked for an answer. Later that night, eerie howls were heard outside, and footsteps on the rooftops awoke him.

The prophet reached for his lantern and lit it, gently walking around the house, checking each room until he came to Miriam's. There he found them huddled together on her bed, with candles lit on the windowpanes.

"Why are you shaking?" asked Feneer.

"Because the old hag of the marsh will get us," said Anna, holding her amulet in her hands for protection against this being in the dark.

"Old hag, eh?" muttered the prophet.

Heavy thuds and the scratching of claws reverberated throughout the house, against the roof and windows, while the animals outside became restless. Terror gripped the family, and they clung to their gods as the laughter of an old woman pierced their ears.

Feneer had had enough, and he told them to wait there in the room until he came back. They begged him not to go, but he left without saying a word. Going outside the door, he stepped into a moonlit, starry night. It was warm outside, with the heavy buzzing of insects in the air. He could see clearly as he walked far enough from the house and spied on the roof a pale, nude wraithlike female with sparse hair, fierce teeth, and glowing green eyes.

"You, witch, will no longer haunt this family!" yelled the prophet.

The hag laughed and cursed him up and down, not knowing with whom she was dealing with. She rushed him as if to frighten him, but he laughed at her as if she was nothing. The hag was furious, and she changed into a coal-black long-clawed wailing banshee, pronouncing death on Feneer. When this had no effect, it charged him in combat, but the warrior grabbed the hag by the maw and said, "The Lord rebuke you," ripping its jaw apart.

Then he battered it senseless with his fists and humbled it with his feet, declaring the Lord's wrath upon it. The screams and gargles of pain were loud and hard on the ears. Inside the house, the family wondered if Feneer was okay, so they came running downstairs and slowly opened the door to see the prophet standing over the ethereal hag with its jaw completely broken and gesturing for mercy. Miriam could not believe her eyes.

Feneer made the hag lay prostrate and humble before him.

"Come," said Feneer. "Come and see what happens to those who defy the living God."

The creature cried out and declared, "The Lord God of heaven, He is the one true God." It then vanished, promising never to bother them again.

With this sight, the woman and her children bowed low before the prophet, trembling and worshipping him in fear.

The prophet bade them to get up hastily for he was not to be worshipped. He then told them about Jehovah, the great and awesome God, the God of all gods, how it was His Spirit and anointing alone that gave him the power to overcome the monster that had plagued them.

He said that if they were to stay protected, they would have to make a choice, of their free will, to follow the Living God and burn and throw away their idols.

Then the prophet leaned over and prayed for them and later anointed them with oil as they repented from their sins and called on the name of the Lord. That morning, he dipped them in the pond to signify the cleansing and taught them concerning the goodness and power of God. God was merciful and kind to them and sent a bird in through a window. It landed on the hand of the prophet and told him the location of her husband, but he did not mention this.

"You understand the fowl?" asked Miriam.

The bird flew out the window. Feneer told them he must depart but would return shortly. The three huddled together as the children sobbed. Then the bird flew back in the window, chirping away, nudging Feneer to follow. Grabbing his staff and covering his head with his hood, he stood and prayed for their protection and told Miriam to wait until he returns. The fowl chirped and chirped, flying overhead as the prophet untethered one of the horses in the stable and followed slowly behind. The mother and her children stood on the porch, wondering where he was going.

The bird led Feneer through beautiful scenery that slowly began to change. Live trees mixed with dead ones stood as far as the eye could see until mostly the dead remained. The ground became too soft and waterlogged for the horse to travel safely, so Feneer decides to trek on foot, telling the horse to wait there. A thick gray mist begins to form as he treads onward. The afternoon seemed to become like night because of the covering of thick swamp fumes and dead vegetation hanging low, blocking out all light. This is indeed a place of evil. The bird flutters violently and tells the prophet he will go no further but directs him the way he should go. Feneer bids the faithful fowl farewell and walks a little farther until he comes to an old roped wooden bridge hanging over a steep gorge.

Slowly he steps across the weak bridge. It swayed, and he did not know if it would support his weight. His staff begins to glow, alerting him of danger. He looks and in the darkness sees winged birdlike shadows perched upon the dead branches above on both

THE ROAD TO CHIDARRA

sides. They didn't move or make a sound, although they did watch him intently as if allowing him to walk through. He comes to a dark cave and tunnel with a hideous face carved on top.

Feneer walks through rats and maggots until he reaches a huge dark, murky, marshy bog void of light and most natural life except things bent on evil, which were corrupted by the eldritch forces that held sway there. A huge three-headed snake slithers past his foot on the muddy bank overlooking the still water. There is an eerie quietness about this place. Mutated insects with long, sharp stingers and deformed wings, attracted to the light of his staff, begin to flutter by his face. Suddenly, through the darkness, a shadowy figure waded through the waters, and Feneer's staff becomes Tempest, shining with power until through the filth and mire, a strange creature emerges.

The thing hobbled out of the water to the muddy shore on all fours and then stood upright on two legs to reveal a tall fat half-swine, half-man thing. Its wiry black hair smelled and was matted with mud and covered with swarming flies. Its snout was long and deformed, with curved sharp tusks and a large tongue that hung sideways out of its mouth.

"Sheath your sword, stranger," said the swine thing. "I am Groak, and I have been sent by the Mistress Nordra, ruler of these parts, to bid you follow. Welcome to the wailing waters of Nordrath."

"Tell your mistress she must come to me for I will go no further in this rotten place," protested Feneer.

"Have it your way," grunted Groak. Then Groak went back on all fours and splashed through the filthy water, disappearing, leaving the prophet alone on shore. After a while, the oars of a boat were heard splashing in the water, getting closer and closer until a large glowing being in the form of an ugly old hag woman with long thin hair, extralong arms, and thin, bony hands stood on the old wooden boat. She was arrayed in a tattered, dirty, yellowish gown, and her head was large, wearing a tiara made of mud on it. In addition, one of her eyes was bigger than the other, and she had the look and smell of decay. One hand had a glistening beautiful silver ring.

Feneer stood silent and grim-faced, in no mood for prattle. In the boat with the wraith were Groak, who manned the oars, and also Uva, the hag who the prophet had punished for harassing Miriam's

23

family. She was filled with terror, her maw still broken and hanging low from the battering Feneer had given it. Gliding overhead were six deformed and fierce, haunting moth-like warriors with long spears, three on each side of the boat, attending to the word of their queen. The boat itself was old, worn, and moss covered.

"I am Mistress Nordra as my herald has stated. There is no reason to stand grim and battle ready, for your Master did send His messenger before you, demanding the bones of the human that we destroyed."

Reaching down and grabbing an old dirty bag, she threw it at the feet of the prophet. He looked in the bag to find the gnawed-on bones of Yohan, the husband of Miriam, with a talisman just like the two children wore. Then the queen, striding out of the ship and floating over the water onto the land, looks down upon the prophet and says, "Let it be known unto you that this man's life was ours by right, for he willingly dabbled in dark arts and was a conjurer that lay in wait to rob and murder unsuspecting travelers of the Argonian forests."

Feneer says nothing, grabs the bag, and walks away from the hag queen and her hosts. Screeches and howls loudly fill the air.

"Be gone, Prophet," screamed Nordra, "for you are most unwelcome here."

Two days later, Miriam and the children are out cleaning the stable when the little bird returns, flying around their heads singing loudly and then swiftly soaring outside. They follow, seeing Feneer riding slowly with the old, dingy bag tied to the horse's saddle. They greet him, wondering of his absence.

"Did you find our father?" begged the children.

Feneer dismounts and unloosens the sack, carrying it over to Miriam. She looks inside and gasps at what she sees. Bruno, the dog, sees the commotion and jumps out the window of the house, leaping into the arms of the prophet.

"Go and take your dog and play for a moment while I speak to your mother, okay, children?" the prophet requests.

The children run off, playing with the dog, and then Feneer tells Miriam the truth.

"Your husband had a dark side unknown to you, milady," says Feneer.

"How so?" asked Miriam with a puzzled look and tears on her face.

"Your beloved would go off in the woods without your knowledge a lot, is that not so?"

"Yes," said the woman.

"And would he also return with items that left you wondering as to how he acquired them?"

Miriam paused and said, "Many a day, Yohan would leave in a hurry, saying it was business of his own and not to ask of the matter. He would return with gifts or things handy he said he obtained from bartering wayfarers or from the lone trading post a day's journey up north. Tell me, what has my husband done?"

Then Feneer pulls the talisman out and gives it her. She turns her head, crying.

"Your husband robbed and plundered lone travelers on the paths in the forest milady. Many he murdered," the prophet said somberly. "But there is more, for he also was a conjurer of spirits and an astrologer, seeking knowledge of the stars through readings and sorcery."

Miriam fell to her knees in disbelief.

"This is why he was taken by the hags of the marsh. He played the fool, trusting in magic and the false gods of this world, only to be destroyed by them, and for his bloodlust, he preyed on the innocent. All this he did behind your back, and so his artifacts of magic must be found and destroyed, and your property cleansed. Otherwise, an open door will remain for further intrusions by dark powers."

Miriam wiped the tears from her eyes and nodded yes to the prophet's commands. Then he gathered the children with their mother and went throughout the property, searching for and gathering all the idols and everything to do with them. They threw them in a pile to be burned, but the Spirit of the Lord told the prophet there was still more hidden. The prophet took his staff, raised it in the air, and prayed, asking God to reveal what hides in secret.

The staff began to shake and pull the prophet through the barn and down a path deep in the woods, with Miriam following behind. There they found a small cave hidden by large bushes on the side of a hill. The cave itself was not very deep, and inside were bones, sprawled out with potions and books of magic next to a fire pit surrounded by stones. Candles, knives, and a board for necromancy lay upon a small altar of stones, with a piece of log to sit on. Idols of devils and dark gods filled the cave, along with incantations with lewd, lustful, and demonic images painted on the walls in blood.

Miriam was horrified and ran back to the barn, weeping. The prophet was about to destroy the cave when the Lord told him to stay his hand. Feneer wondered to himself why the Lord would say so when Miriam returned with the bag of bones, talisman, and her children. Then she said, "My children must know the truth."

She took them by the hand and explained to them that their father did witchcraft and conjured demons and that the Lord told her to tell them the truth of the matter. Afterward, she took the bag and threw it in the cave when suddenly a voice thundered in the clouds.

God said, "Woman, because you repented two nights ago and believed on Me after the word of My prophet and because you gathered all the idols and even the bones of your dead husband as an unclean thing to be burned up in the fire, I, the Lord, shall finish the cleansing of your land by fire. Then you shall know there is a God who rules and created all things that judges the earth."

God commanded that they run up to the top of the hill on the path when dark clouds appeared and strong winds began to blow, shaking and causing a howl in the trees. The tall grass flailed helplessly while dust from the dirt path clouded their vision. Thunder sounded in the heavens and arcs of lightning crackled from the sky into the cave and destroyed it, leaving a smoldering mound of ash and molten rock.

Fear gripped their hearts as they ran back toward the farm, where they heard the screaming of evil spirits in horror and saw the mound of idols and things of magic burnt in a pyre of smoke and flame. Then everyone knelt down prostrate before the Lord while the animals fled from the presence of the Most High. There they stayed lying before Him until darkness began to fall.

Then the prophet bade them to rise, and he took them and again prayed for them and for himself because none could sleep that night for fear of the Lord. The next morning, Feneer went out, found large stones, and carried them as if they were but pebbles, placing them one on top of the other, making an altar for the Lord where the burning of the accursed things took place. Nothing was left, not even ash or soot on the ground, for the Lord sent a wind in the night to blow it all away, but the ground around it was still singed to remind them what the Lord had done.

When the altar was completed, he called them, and there he prepared a burnt offering unto the Lord and taught them the holiness of God. He also told them many stories that he had seen and read to them from the scrolls of the prophets and Torah, the Holy word of God. After many days, the Lord moved him to prepare to depart on toward his assignment west. Feneer called them over to him to bid them farewell. Tears were shed by the family. Then the Spirit of the Lord moved upon Miriam, and she began to prophesy, foretelling of dangers that lay ahead for the prophet, saying that he must be obedient, strong, and encouraged at the word of the Lord.

Then the Lord spoke and told Miriam that she was to be separate and consecrated unto him to stand in the gap as a door of hope and light, exposing the darkness in that region. He Himself would teach her of holiness and His ways. At His word, she reached into the prophet's bag around his waist, told him to kneel, anointed him with oil that ran down his face, and laid hands upon him, blessing him on his journey. Her children bowed their heads, worshipping silently behind her. Then Miriam called them to the stall, unlatched one of the horses, and led it to the house, telling him to grab his things and be ready to mount quickly.

After all was prepared, he mounted the steed with his sack and the golden bag tied upon the saddle. Then the prophetess said, "'Thus,' says the Lord, 'you are to leave, but the golden bag and all therein must stay. For I have other purposes for them. I will establish my name once again throughout the land and make war, casting judgment on the false gods and those who follow them to their ruin and utter desolation. As for these here, they are in my care, and they shall be established as trees, bearing fruit for my glory to the blessing of others who shall call on my name.'"

Then the prophet removes his hair band and takes off his cloak tunic and his shoes, leaving only his pants, and bows before the Lord. They see the stripes and wounds upon his body. Strong, large, and well-built, he is still a grim warrior born. His locks dangle upon his back and the ground as he spreads his arms out and lays flat, face-first in the dirt, and says, "Thank you, Lord, for showing mercy not only to this family but others who venture in this dark land and for establishing Your Name and Holiness once again throughout. Blessed be your name, for this shall be called holy ground and not accursed any longer.

"Many are the faithful who serve You in their own lands across the earth, and they have places to worship You in truth and reverence. Now this place shall be blessed, for You will visit these peoples, teaching righteousness and repentance to those You love and have shown mercy to. Praise be to Thee, o God, the Most High and Creator of heaven and earth!"

Then Miriam saw his deep love for God and said, "I sensed at our meeting you were an honorable man, safe around my children. God bless you with a family and godly friends." Miriam hurried and gathered fruit bread and water in a bundle for his journey.

Feneer smiled, nodded, picked himself up, and went over to the red steed, unlatching the golden bag. Giving it to the woman, he told her to keep the bag in a safe place and seek the Lord with the prayers and fasting that he had taught her and that the Lord was her strength and redeemer.

Then he said, "Remember, be not afraid of evil, for the Lord shall protect you, and if you are tormented by foul spirits, you must call on the name of the Lord with His word and in His name, and He will send his angels to protect you. His Holy Spirit shall deliver you. Demon spirits and all false gods are terrified of the One True God, answering only to Him and not good luck charms, talismans, incantations, or any occult objects. These things attract them and bring misery oppression, poverty, and illness to those who own them. Never carry a conversation with them or seek their knowledge for they always lie and will seduce you to ruin, and beware of monsters such as the hags and other creatures of the Nephilim. They are terrible and dreadful, and for these is my mantle given."

After this, Feneer hugs them tightly, thanking them for their kindness and for bringing him joy. Then he mounts his steed, departing from their sight by the glare of the golden sun.

THREE

SUFFER THE LITTLE ONES

The land indeed has its perils, but it is also full of wonder and mystery. For further west but toward the south near the ruins of Undim live a quiet folk called the Ciqala. They are forest dwellers of many different shades who make their homes in the hollows and tops of the large trees that inhabit the timber. Some tree homes are large and fancy while others are small, simple, and quaint. It was a true village in the sky that belies the equally impressive homes unseen below the forest floor in torch-lit dens and tunnels under the ground.

These folk are small, averaging three and a half or so feet in height, with bright eyes, full cheeks, and are born in different shades of color yet live in harmony. Their eyes are keen in the dark, and their ears pick up the slightest sounds in the timber. They are a shy but happy folk who love to sing songs, make music, and have feasts that keep the heart merry. At certain times of the season, the fruit called jujala falls to the ground, then ferments quickly, making a thick sweet, tangy wine called juja. Indeed, they love to make beers, wines, and ales of many kinds that they trade from time to time with far-off villages.

One day, a young Ciqala named Faolan, along with his friends Egan and Goban, were gathering berries, trapping rabbits for supper, and enjoying their time in the timber.

"I bet I catch the biggest fattest rabbit," said Faolan.

"Bet you don't," said Goban, chewing on a piece of bark. "In fact, I bet you your sack of berries that I catch the biggest."

While these two challenged one another, Egan quietly listened for the rustle of leaves on the forest floor. He saw a rabbit in a clearing eating a blade of grass. While Faolan and Goban walked on, he sat back slowly and silently pulled out a leather sling and a smooth stone.

The large rabbit seemed not to notice him and his friends.

Gently he put the stone in the sling and began to twirl it until he released it, hitting the rabbit dead-on. The creature ran in a circle until it dropped dead. Egan ran to the clearing with lush green grass and picked up his prize, smirking while his friends marched along, unaware. Then he pranced up to them, not saying a word, and showed them the fat furry meal he had just caught while they still argued who would get the finest catch.

"Where did you get that?" they both shouted.

"You were busy talking while I was busy listening," said Egan. "It was in that clearing, minding its own business, and the two of you passed right by it. I noticed it as it rustled some leaves on the ground, and there you go."

"He's awful big, isn't he?" said Goban. "Did you see any more?"

"I didn't see, but we can go back and check," said Egan. "Maybe there is a nest nearby."

With that thought, the three friends ran back to the clearing and searched but found no rabbit's nest. They went to the other side of the clearing and through more woods until they came to a muddy, rocky field with tall gray grass and a lone cave with strange but faint sounds coming from it.

The cave was large and dark, with big stones sprawled about its entrance. A rancid smell spewed from it as they walked a little closer to see what was inside. Faolan noticed bones of animals on the ground picked clean. Then Goban slipped on a group of slick stones and fell face-first to the ground. It is then that he notices that they are not stones but skulls of animals and men with chewed-up, bloody clothes spat on the ground. Terror strikes his heart. The other two pick him up and notice the gruesome scene, and they each hear a stir in the cave.

"Let's get out of here," whispers Faolan.

The three tiptoe out of the cave as fast as they can, leaving behind berries and rabbit alike until they reach the path to their village called Abbonwood.

Out of breath and shaken, they rest under an oak tree, trying to quell the fear inside them.

"That sound was not the cave. It was someone or something breathing," said Goban.

"Wh-what do you think it was?" asked Egan.

"Maybe the cave trolls have returned."

"But there hasn't been a sighting of cave trolls around these parts for years," protested Faolan.

"I don't know, but we have to alert the village," said Egan. "Our people could be in danger."

The three friends gather their strength and run off to the village as fast as they can. As they approach Abbonwood, the sound of music and dancing is heard, with drums, flutes, the timbrel, and the lyre. Leaves gently fall to the ground as the little people dance on the trees, shaking the branches, playing instruments, and drinking ale. On the ground, the smoky smell of roast fowl and piglet on fire spits permeates the air. Children play as women make sport, dancing in lines with one another.

Underneath, in their burrows, play continues as their fellows above have a good old time with one another. The children were playing hide-and-seek in the tunnels lit with torch and glow root, running belowground in the forest, evading their mates, when Faolan, Goban, and Egan appear out of breath and fall to the ground.

The celebration stops above as the people see the fright in their eyes. A bearded, stout, bowlegged fellow with a pipe and ale mug pushed his way through the crowd. He was of darker skin, with curly hair, and he leaned over to question them. It was Cerin, the father of Faolan.

"My son, what's wrong? What has you and your friends so frightened?" asked Cerin.

The people underground notice the silence overhead and begin to come out, asking what transpires. Surrounded by villagers, the three friends tell their tale to the elders, who send out five scouts to investigate the claims of the youth. The Ciqala are not warriors but are a peaceful folk, albeit there be some of stout heart who are good hunters and handy with a bow and dagger. Watchmen stand guard with torches lighting the village while all others venture inside their tree houses and burrows underneath until the danger is surmised.

High in the tallest tree is a large house that extends outward, overlooking the village on sturdy, thick leafy branches. Inside the palace is the home of the village elder and chief whose name is Arno. Arno is reddish-skinned, with yellow eyes and a long white beard. His hat is green and slightly pointed at the top. A large brim around that shades his visage. He sits on a wooden high-backed chair laced with gold and precious stones. By his side is his bride, Attila, who sits on her throne, which was covered in silver with precious stones and stained glass leaves covering its headrest as a shroud. There are four smaller thrones on each side, with male elders next to Arno and females next to Attila.

Around the palace, lanterns adorn its walls, illuminating it throughout. Art and various manner of décor fancy up this place, with guards placed at each entrance of the stairwells inside the tree and on the ground. Also in the trees and on the ground in secret are lookouts placed along the perimeter of the village. It is now nighttime, and the village is on edge. Doors are locked tight as the little people shut themselves in for safety in their tree homes. Underground entrances are sealed with stones and earth to conceal their presence while doors are locked, keeping the little peoplein their dens as most candles and torches are put out.

Arno ponders the situation, considering that the five have not returned as of yet. Thinking evil has befallen them, he sends for two of his swiftest and stealthiest couriers to seek aid from the kingdom of Chidarra. Chidarra's King Dothan has ever been friendly to the little folk as they trade wine and forest herbs for livestock and tools from their smiths.

Guards holding torches go to the house of Barran and knock on the red-painted door.

"Who is it?" cried Barran from within.

"You are wanted by Arno, the chief, for a special purpose courier," said a guard. "Come and make haste."

Barran holds his head in his hands and closes his eyes, wishing he did not hear the command to come before the chief when he hears another knock, louder this time.

"Come and bring attire to run swiftly," said the guard.

Barran grabs a small sack, puts it on his back, and goes with the guards. Then at the palace, he meets Ivan, who kneels in front of the elders. Then Barran also kneels as the queen speaks.

"You two must make haste and take the underground passages as far as you can until you reach the kingdom of Chidarra and King Dothan. There, tell him we need aid against an unknown threat that feeds upon our people."

"Make haste," said Arno, "and may the divine guide you."

The two couriers nod and then run out of the tree palace, leaping from tree limb to tree limb until they reach the bottom. Then they dart swiftly to the edge of the village and enter a large hollow tree stump leading to a secret underground entrance and whisk off into the darkness. Moments later, screams are heard aboveground, and the shaking of the earth causes dirt and debris to collapse upon the underground burrows. Many are trapped or crushed by the weight of the earth and stone. Aboveground, the crashing of trees and screams of horror fill the air.

Chaos rules as the Ciqala run for their lives in every direction. Inside, the den of Cerin begins to crumble, and he grabs his son and pushes him out the door as it splinters and breaks apart. Cerin tries to follow, but the entrance collapses and crushes him, leaving his son Faolan alone to escape aboveground. There he sees Goban and Egan running in circles, not knowing where to go or where the danger comes from. There is madness in the night, and when Faolan cries out to them, they follow into the darkness, trying to escape the unknown death that lurks around them.

Five days later, a cloaked figure rides silently upon a red steed down the path to Abbonwood. There he finds nothing but ruin. Little homes in trees are broken down and destroyed, those lairs that dwell underground dug up. Tiny blood-soaked, chewed-up, and half-eaten clothes cover the forest floor and hang from a few trees, but not a single body was found.

Who were these poor little people? he pondered within. *Why did this happen, and who did it? Was it a war that took place, or perhaps some natural disaster destroyed them?* None were alive to tell the tale of the village's demise. The ground is marred and undone.

Seeing what seems to be the leader's home because of its splendor, Feneer leaps off his horse and, with staff in hand, walks near the ruinous heap of Arno's palace. No bodies could be found. No life was left in this place. The prophet looked at the trees to see many of them knocked over or twisted as if by a great force. Sorrow enters his heart for the victims of this village when he goes over to a small stone well and pulls up some water for his horse. Then he sits down and begins to pray to God for guidance.

After a while, Feneer hears the faint sound of movement. Two little figures appear from behind toppled and crushed trees. The prophet senses them but does not open his eyes. A third figure grabs his staff, which was leaning against the wall, and darts off in the woods. The other two pull out daggers and confront the prophet, who still does not open his eyes.

"Who are you, cloaked one?" yelled Faolan. "Answer me, or so help me, we shall gut you where you stand."

Feneer does not say a word, nor does he open his eyes. Then Egan comes around, holding the staff in his hand.

"Look, look, I have his staff!" cried Egan. The staff was wood carved and braided together in three as a three-bonded cord. On it were words carved in an unknown language, and the top of the staff had three faceless creatures with a set of wings, each facing the center, making a triangle.

"A wizard's staff, no doubt," said Goban. "He must have cast a spell and destroyed our people."

"Or summoned whatever foul beast that did!" cried Faolan.

After hearing them call him a wizard, Feneer opened his eyes and said, "I am no wizard." Then he stood up and gently asked for his staff. The trio backed away with tears in their eyes, frightened by the mysterious figure that stood before them. Feneer called them over and, bowing before them, asked, "Is this your village?"

"Yes," said Egan, still holding the staff.

"I am very sorry," said the prophet.

When the trio heard this, they could no longer contain their grief, and they fell to their knees and wept out loud. There they mourned as the prophet sat in silence, not taking the staff from, Egan allowing them their space to grieve with no interruption. Indeed, he understood what they were going through.

Then Egan, still clutching the staff, arose from the ground and walked over to the prophet, returning what belonged to him.

Feneer said, "It is not good that we stay here for it will be dark soon enough. Is there a place where we can lodge and speak of this matter?"

"There is a hidden lair that our folk used to hide from rock trolls in ages past," said Faolan. "That is where we hid ourselves these five days since we left in the terror of the night."

"Let us be off then, before night comes and hinders our trek," said Feneer.

There they went, the prophet and his little companions of the wood. Feneer went on foot, walking with his staff, and allowed the trio of Ciqala to ride his horse, for he felt pity for these tiny creatures. The forest floor was laden with pine nettles and sparse mushrooms covering the landscape. The rubble of ancient buildings sunken deep in the earth and covered by the forest haunts this place, relics of Undim's outposts from a forgotten age, a time long before the kingdom of Itvihiland had yet risen. It is now getting dark, and Feneer looks around to see tree leaves everywhere sparkle with different colors, illuminating the forest.

"Beautiful," he said.

Faolan called for the horse to stop. "We're here." He sighed.

A large tree with several others embedded along the side of a steep hill that has no path is where they stop. The horse was tired and needed rest, along with everyone else, for it was hard walking up, down, and through the forest hillside.

"Do you see where we shall lodge, stranger?" asked Egan.

The prophet said no, daring not to use his staff to reveal the hidden lair so as not to frighten them. The trio leaped off the horse, reached between the roots on the ground, and pulled a lever that opens a pathway in the hillside. The opening is big enough for them but not for the horse, so the prophet ties it up to a tree and then enters the ancient lair.

The entrance is cloaked with root and stone. Vines cover the earthen floor that reaches back into the hillside. The prophet has to crouch over to avoid hitting his head on the root-laden ceiling. The trio slowly walk until they come to a room where it is warm and cozy. Fresh leaves cover the floor, along with brown flat stones to rest their heads on. The Ciqala can see well in the dark, but not so much the prophet. He holds his peace and does not use his staff to light the way, lest they think him a magician and fear.

Then they tell him their names and the story of the bones and sounds from the cave and then of the unknown horror they later fled in the dark. They said they may be the only ones left alive that escaped or there may be others hiding in the forest who may have reached friendly regions. They did not know of the two couriers sent to seek aid before them.

"Pardon our rudeness," said Faolan. Then he reached up and pulled on the small roots that dangled overhead, and a faint amount of light gleamed from them. The roots sparkled like the leaves, and they were abundant in these parts of the wood. Feneer had forgotten about these things, and he smiled as he watched his companions get comfortable.

Looking at them, he marveled at the different shades of skin they each carried. For Faolan was brown toned, but Egan was fair skinned, and still Goban was of a yellow complexion.

"Where are you from?" asked Goban.

"I am from an ancient land many leagues from here across the great oceans to the east," said Feneer.

"And how old are you?" asked Egan.

"Old enough to see many places, peoples, and things, things of awe and beauty and other things best left unsaid," said Feneer.

"Have you seen creatures of magic and fought any battles or seen any to speak of?" they asked.

"I have fought many battles and seen many great beings of good and evil. I am Feneer, and there is more that I must tell you, but now is not the time." Then the prophet removes his cloak and begins to sing a poem of mourning for the little creatures that are of such heavy heart.

"O cry, little ones, and mourn your loss of kin and friend alike. With heavy hearts, your tears must flow before the sun will rise. There is no shame for feeling pain that gnaws from deep within. There is a Redeemer who loves and spares. Yea, cast all your cares on Him.

"He sits upon His throne above, for He is the Divine Judge. With mercy and love, His hands have made the earth, the moon, and sun. He is the Great and awesome God, whom all men should love and fear, the Lord of Hosts, the Great I AM. In mystery, He is near. Now rest, little ones, for He hears your cries and shall wipe away your tears."

The prophet sings the song as the trio shed a few tears and, like children seeking comfort, throw themselves upon the startled stranger, who holds back tears of his own. Then the prophet begins to recite Psalm 23 quietly, so the word of God may refresh and bring healing to their broken spirits. The little ones cry themselves to sleep in the arms of the prophet, who gently lays each of them down on the leaf-bedded floor. Then he takes his cloak gently, covers them, and falls asleep.

Late the next morning, the three friends wake up to find themselves alone in the hidden lair. Perplexed, they stumble to the entrance and pull a root on the ground that opens it to find Feneer sitting down on a rock, eating warm meal cakes and drinking a flagon of water. A warm fire crackles in a clearing he put together with three stones for them to sit upon.

"Ah, there you are. Good morning, my little companions," said Feneer with a bright smile. "Hurry, my friends, and gather wood for the fire and for cooking over the fire," said the prophet.

"Where did you get this food from?" asked Faolan.

"Hurry, I say, little ones, hurry!" shouted the prophet. "I sense they are almost here."

Suddenly shadows are seen high above through the trees. The small trio cannot believe their eyes when they see three very large eagles, exceedingly fierce, glide down and drop three large salmon before Feneer. The little ones run in fear behind the trees, breathing heavily but looking on in amazement.

"Be not afraid, little ones, they won't harm you," shouted the prophet.

The three friends creep from behind the trees and walk behind the prophet for protection. The eagles are large, with huge talons and sharp beaks. Their eyes glare at them with their wings extending fully as they walk toward the prophet, chirping and whistling. He responds by nodding his head and waves them off, with the birds flying away majestically.

"This is why I hurried you to find wood," said Feneer. Then he grabbed the fish and gave one to each of them while they just stared at him, wondering what manner of man can speak to and understand the animals of the forest. "Now go ahead and clean your food to roast in the fire so you can eat," said the prophet, smiling. "The Most High has blessed us with food and drink to start our day. He wants you to know that He loves you and also that He is watching you."

The three friends look at one another with their mouths agape and run off to clean their fish. After eating the fish, they rest in the cool of the forest as the prophet tells them about the Lord, His God, and how He created all things and that he loves good and hates evil. After this, he instructs them to get ready for they must return to Abbonwood, their village.

"Why, sir?" asked Egan. "For there is nothing to behold there but heartache and death."

"The eagles told me the Lord desires us go back," said Feneer. "I shall do as He commands me."

Then the prophet puts out the fire and mounts them back on his horse, heading back to the village. Meanwhile a band of soldiers bearing the banner of Chidarra, with bows, shields, swords, spears, axes, and light armor trek through the forest toward Abbonwood on horseback. With them are the two couriers, Barran and Ivan, leading the way. The band of warriors gets to the village first and sees the devastation. Ivan and Barran begin to weep bitterly as the warriors remove their helmets, bowing their heads out of respect. Then Ivan and Barran run to their homes to find them gone and totally undone.

The captain of this guard of forty was a man named Luic. He was a proud, valiant warrior and a faithful leader. His host would willingly die for him for esteemed him as a true warrior who would do the same for them.

"Look about and search for survivors," beckoned Luic. Then he walked over and knelt on one knee to comfort the two Ciqala in mourning.

Out of the clearing, walking with his staff, appears Feneer, who startles a soldier, who raises his bow and orders the prophet to slowly come with him. Then two other soldiers raise spears from behind and lead him to Luic.

"Who are you, and what are you doing here?" demanded the captain.

Feneer says nothing when a soldier removes his hood and strikes him on the cheek, demanding he answer the word of his captain.

Again, the prophet says nothing when they remove his shoulder bag and look through it to find a small dagger, flint rocks, oils medicines, and a small leather book with strange writing and symbols. The soldiers look at one another and then back at Feneer, who calmly stands alone among angry men and Ciqala alike. They notice him slowly look behind as if searching for something.

Then the captain steps forth and says, "I ask you one last time, stranger, who are you, and what are you doing here?"

"I'd say he's a wizard to look about him sir," said one of his soldiers.

They mumble in agreement on this. The prophet shrugs his shoulders, takes a deep breath, and says, "Of truth, I am no conjurer of spells, nor am I a being of magic. I am a prophet of an ancient order called the Eitan Navi."

"Prophet, are you. So tell us, prophet, what shall be your fate if you don't reveal to us what you're doing here?" asked Luic.

Then running up the path frantically are the three Ciqala, with the red steed galloping behind them.

"Stay your swords and unhand him," said Goban. "He is our friend." Then the two couriers run up to their kinfolk and embrace. Ivan tells Luic that it's okay because they are friends. Luic orders the release of Feneer but watches him with a keen eye, fearing he may still be a sorcerer.

"We thought no one survived and we were all that was left," said Goban.

"So did we," said Barran. "It is so very good to see you all."

With tears of joy, they embrace until the dark reality again hits that they are all that is left. Again, sadness shrouds deeply upon them.

"Did anyone here see what laid waste to your village? Have you any knowledge of the enemy we face?" asked Endrr, the captain's hand.

The Ciqala all say the same thing. They saw nothing but heard the crashing of trees and felt the shaking of the earth. What burned within their memories are the death screams of their people and the terror of that night.

"Whatever it was it had to be massive, looking at the extent of the damage," said a soldier.

Luic nodded in agreement. A scout looked at the ground and saw large markings but could not make them out.

"Sir, come look at this," called Endrr. The indentations looked like large footprints with four wide toes and animal prints, also large, of an unknown origin.

"Have you ever seen prints like these?" asked Luic to the Ciqala.

"No, never," they said. Everyone looked on, wondering just what they were dealing with. Endrr looked at Feneer and said, "So, prophet, can you not divine and tell us what we face?"

Feneer slowly bowed his head as if concentrating or listening to something as everyone stares at him. Then he nods his head and opens his eyes when Endrr and Luic again rudely demand answers.

Feneer looked at them and then at the five Ciqala and said to the captain, "You are a good man, Luic of Chidarra, and a faithful servant of your king. You are to go and confront this enemy, and fear not, for the Lord has given them into your hands. If they ask for mercy, then make them swear to leave this place and trouble its inhabitants no more. And if not, then wipe them out, do you understand?"

"And by whose authority do you say these things, prophet?" asked Luic. "Shall we listen to you on a whim and end up as this village and its people did? Shall we trust the murmurings of a wanderer in the wilds with his wooden staff and sack of goods?"

Then the prophet loses his patience, strikes his staff on the ground, and causes a mild tremor that shakes the ground so that all but he loses their footing. Then he raises both hands high and covers his face with his hood. His eyes begin to glow white when he says, "Listen, and listen well to my words, man of Chidarra, I am Feneer, servant of the Lord God, Creator of heaven and earth, and I am on a mission most urgent. It would behoove you and your men to heed my edicts for indeed my patience wears thin and my wrath is terrible. I am no wizard, nor am I your enemy."

Then the tremor stops, and all step back before the prophet in fear. "Arise and listen carefully. You are to go and confront this foe, for I, at first, thought to punish them myself, but the Lord has sent me on a different path. After you have defeated your enemy, you are to take the five Ciqala to their kin tribes, where they can dwell with their people. After this, return to your kingdom, where I shall meet you to have council with your sire."

"No, we don't want to leave you," cried his three little friends.

"You must be obedient and do as the Lord commands. Remember what I told you? That he shall care for you?" said Feneer, smiling at them.

"We do as you say," said Luic, bowing low in respect. "Forgive us for our disrespect of one who is a prophet of the gods of the heavens."

"*God* of the heavens, said Feneer sternly, "and all is forgiven, my friends and favored of the Most High." He walks over to the edge of the village and the damaged pathway that leads to the cave where the trio saw the bones. The prophet turns and blesses the brave company on their journey, for he knew they may encounter other trials to make them faint on the way.

His little friends clutch his garment and hold him close, not wanting to let him go when he blesses them in the name of the Lord three times. After this, he sends out a strange call in the forest and tells the men to wait. A large black dire wolf with red eyes strides before the prophet and licks him. The soldiers draw swords cautiously, looking for the rest of the pack as the wolf goads them to follow.

"He will lead you to your enemy and, if necessary, aid you in battle," said Feneer, pointing his finger at Luic.

"Keep the little ones safe, and if I do not meet you in your kingdom ahead of you, then wait for me, and tell no one of my presence until I arrive. This is an evil land with hidden dangers and beings I have not dealt with before, but the Lord is my strength," said Feneer. "Be brave and do not delay, for God shall lead you in battle," the prophet demanded.

While looking at the captain, he said, "Do you trust my words, Luic, son of Alphor?"

"I do," said the captain, looking at him and wondering how he knew his father's name. "I don't know why, but I do."

"At the time of battle, you and your men shall shout for God and Chidarra, this shall be your war cry, do you understand?" said Feneer.

Looking puzzled, Luic stares at his men.

Then he waved them on in single file as they rode their horses, following the huge black dire wolf that strode effortlessly through the wood, with the Ciqala riding in the middle of the pack. The prophet knelt down and silently prayed, preparing for the unknown and greater dangers he may face. After praying, he calls his horse, puts on his shoulder bag, and with his sack of goods tied to the saddle, rides west with the swiftness as thick gray clouds begin to form overhead, perhaps as an omen of things to come.

Slowly and tediously, the band of forty warriors with their five woodland friends follows the wolf while being on alert for anything dangerous around them. The forest was strangely quiet and foreboding with the wreckage of trees and foliage along the path. Something very destructive filled with rage and hate swathed through here. The closer the Ciqala get to the cave, the more afraid they become. There is a dank smell in the air as the wolf looks back to see if they still follow until it reaches the oak tree that the three friends rested under. Then it starts to run swiftly on the path, with the horses speeding up behind it until finally they reach the clearing where the rabbit was found.

The air becomes heavy with moisture as a light drizzle of rain begins to fall from the gray sky above. Onward and bravely, they march in single file through the thick woods on the other side of the clearing and up a rocky dirt path as raindrops pelt the tree leaves on their way to the ground. The smell gets worse as they continue through darkened and damp forest where more damage to the land and bones are seen spewed about. Finally they come to another clearing, a large muddy field full of rocks and tall grass that leads to the ominous cave. Luic commands the troop to hold as he looks at the situation before them. Then he dismounts and walks slowly toward the cave, observing more bones and carcasses that are sprawled about. The smell is horrid, and the sight brings a sense of dread upon him. Slowly he waves for the rest of the troop to dismount and follow his lead while the Ciqala hold the horses. Armed they are for battle, with swords shields and spears, bows, maces, crossbows, curved daggers, and axes. All is quiet around them, save only for the howl of the wind that blows through the grass, increasing with intensity, and the sound of the rain that begins to pelt the landscape.

Heavier still become the dark gray clouds above them when deep gargling sounds are heard coming from within the cave. The horses become restless as the little ones herd them by the trees and climb upon their branches, looking for a better view.

"Do you hear that sound, Captain?" says Endrr.

"Indeed," answers Luic. "Men, ready your weapons and be hungry for battle. And above all, may courage endure within your breasts."

The men ready themselves for an unknown foe. The ground begins to shake beneath them, and their eyes bulge wide open. For what they see defies description.

Large hairy croggoth ogres ramble forth from the cave. They are twice the size of men, with an extended bottom maw and large jagged, edged teeth. Their heads are full of thick black hair that reaches down the whole of the back, as a lion's mane. They have large pointed ears and big lumpy noses, with hair coming out of their nostrils. Their eyes are none but deep black sockets covered over with flesh while their hands are large and rough-hewn, with thick claws that extend outward. They snarl and sniff the air like dogs, picking up a scent as their bellies bulge from feasting.

Broad and boney spines protrude from out of their hunched backs and arms, with overgrown four-toed feet that helps them keep their balance. They hold thick chains with Mwogg rats larger than bulls with spines that stick out of their backs. Long sharp teeth and claws they sport for battle, with coal black eyes that pierce the soul. Their tails are thick and long while their hair is coarse and sharp. Twelve march forth from the cave holding clubs of wood and sharp stone, uttering words in an unknown guttural language.

Luic gathers his men and tells them to hold a flank between them. Uneasiness begins to grip their hearts when Luic shouts, "Remember the word of the prophet, we are to fight and fear not, for his God has giving us the victory."

Hearing those words the ogres laugh and let loose the rats on them. Endrr shouts for a volley of arrows that rain upon a few of the vermin, making them shriek, but they keep charging. Another volley flies, but still closer they come. Howling is heard through the battle as three dire wolf packs charge from the wood, entering the fray from different directions, led by the large black wolf and attacking their foes. Then shouts of battle come from the men as they wage war on the enemy.

The ogres respond with rage and enter the battle, swinging their clubs at the smaller warriors before them. The rains increase, causing the foul cavern dwellers to lose their footing and not comprehend from where their foes attack. For they see not but go about by smell and hearing. Still the battle is theirs, for great is their power and size, and when a few men barely escape from being eaten alive, that sight causes doubt in the hearts of the soldiers. The foul ogres start getting the upper hand until Faolan remembered the words of Feneer. Out of the tree and off he went into the fray, looking for Luic at the frantic protest of his kin. He finds the captain hacking away at the legs of an ogre who misses him with his club.

"What are you doing here?" shouted Luic. "Get back before your blood is on my hands."

"Remember, sir, what the prophet told you. He said to shout for God and Chidarra, and the battle would be won," screamed Faolan.

When the captain heard this, at first he doubted the merit of the saying. Nevertheless, with the battle in the balance, he had nothing to lose and began halfheartedly to shout those words. Then the camp shouted them until they noticed the tide of the battle begin to turn. Their courage started to rise.

Then the rains pounded harder on the combatants until the ground underneath the ogres began to soften and become as deep mire until they sank more than waist deep in the ground. The more they struggled, the deeper they sank, but the men kept their footing.

Seeing this, the men began to cry louder, "For God and Chidarra, for God and Chidarra" until they began to slay the ogres with sword and ax by hacking them to death. Archers shoot arrows upon them, puncturing their thick bloody gray hides until most cried in agony, going limp and lifeless. Those of stouter heart struggled in the mire, flailing their chains and clubs, throwing stones at the warriors, but to no avail, for their doom was certain. The four other wood dwellers leaped from the trees and ran up to the last three ogres who still had faint life left and took out their daggers and exacted revenge upon them for the sake of their fallen people. Cutting and stabbing deep until no life was left. The dire wolves overcame the Mwogg rats and slew them, chasing the few that remained deep into the cave. After the slaughter was finished, the band of wolves looked upon the men, howling victory, and slowly walked off into the forest, leaving behind the black wolf.

Luic stepped forth, saluting it as the wolf turned and howled, disappearing into the wood. The rains began to subside, and the gray skies cleared, revealing carnage and the deaths of their foes.

The ground shook, and the soldiers ran for cover. The Lord caused a tremor that closed the entrance off from the rest of the clan that fled deep underground in terror. The host of ogres that fell before them that day, along with their pets and whatever still dwelled within the cavernous hillside, dared not return to haunt that wood and its inhabitants again.

The soldiers gathered their composure and silently looked at one another, saying nothing until Endrr tapped Luic on the shoulder and said, "Who will believe us of this tale when we barely believe it ourselves?"

Luic turns and nods his head in agreement as Endrr shouts for the men to be at attention and to give account of their well-being. All are battle weary and in great wonder of what happened before their eyes, but they are all healthy and accounted for. Not one person lost their life or was even injured. All noted to a man that the battle was in doubt until they cried out in the name of Feneer's God as they looked upon the monstrous foes that lay lifeless in front of them.

Then Luic knelt before the Ciqala and comforted them for the terrors and loss they endured at the hands of the ogres, showing compassion to them. The Ciqala looked with hatred at the ogres and their giant vermin.

Ivan said, "Your friend, the stranger, said our foes would be delivered to our hands. He truly must be a prophet and his God real because there is no way to explain the rains only affecting the ground around the ogres, leaving them helpless and sinking like quicksand."

"Not to mention the quake that sealed the cave and the dire wolves that came to our aid," said Barran, "and not one man was lost when we were hopelessly outmatched. There is no telling how many more terrors would have come from that dreaded cave, let alone the ones we fought."

Luic pats Goban on the head and points to the blue sky and says, "I thought it foolishness to cry out to an unknown God for aid, and if not for the fact that the battle was going grim, I wouldn't have at all. I don't, or at least didn't, believe the gods, if there were any, answered the cries of mere men, for I have traveled to and fro and seen my fair share of pain, misery, and death to doubt the charity of gods or to believe in them. I have not seen much compassion from gods, nor from man one to another to make me believe in the greater good. But we all saw with our own eyes strange things today, and none of us can deny that fact."

Then Luic gathered his men close and said, "I myself am not much of religious sort, but if this God is real, I think it wise that we should acknowledge its presence."

Everyone looked around at one another, unsure of what to do or say. Then Goban requested if it was okay that he say a little prayer, and the men agreed.

Bowing his head, with everyone following, he said, "God of Feneer, whatever your name may be, if you are real and are as potent as your prophet said, then we give thanks to you for aiding our bows, our axes, our swords, shields, and hands against a great evil that took the lives of our kinfolk and destroyed our village. Moreover, we give thanks for sending the rains that turned the ground so that they sank in the mud and for sending fierce wolves to fight with us. We all know the battle was lost until we cried your name, O God of heaven and earth, I don't know what else to say, but I speak for all when I say, we salute you." Then all beat their chests with heads bowed in silent homage.

After this, their mood lightened, and they spoke to one another about the victory and how bravely they fought the ogres but mostly how the prophet's words were true and wondering about him. Who was this mysterious stranger who came from nowhere, and who is his God, who aided them in battle, for they never faced a foe such as these beings before. If not for the spoils of victory, meaning the two large clubs tied to the horses, who would believe their story? Then after much debate and kidding one another of who did the most damage to the Croggoth ogres, they made their way back from that dreadful graveyard, with its vile dead sunken in the grassy mud, calling it the cave of woe.

Finding a place to camp under the cover of the forest, they made fires and ate of their provisions, resting for the night. The next morning, they gathered their belongings, mounted their horses, and made haste, riding northeast toward the village of Junayd, home of the mountain Ciqala in the lands of Imsdarr. Unknown to them, a stealthy figure evades detection in the dark wood, following behind, intent on not being seen.

FOUR

POWERS OF WIND, WATER,
AND A TOUCH OF EDEN

Days later, on horseback, Feneer emerges from Argonia, where he enters the valley of Sondirra. Still his mind wanders, thinking of the little companions that he left behind, but he does not inquire to the Lord about it. All he knows is that the Holy Spirit has led him this way, but the reason remains a mystery. The sunlight feels good as its rays warm his body. He rides until he reaches windy and treacherous hillside paths named Vudis Hills, where he dismounts and leads his horse by hand until they reach a plateau.

There he sits down upon a rock and rests to soak up more of the sun. All is still for a while, but inside he feels a slight uneasiness. He cannot tell what it is, but there is something not right here. To one not adept to spiritual things, it would seem as if all was well, but not to those sensitive to the unseen realms. Still he relaxes, for rest is needed, and he was weary from travel.

While looking up at the sunny sky laced with white puffy clouds, he smiles and embraces this quiet, contemplative moment. Then he notices a smaller cloud in the distance that seems to sit still, unmoved by the wind. Closing his eyes, he's unaware that the cloud ominously approaches. Suddenly a strong wind gust startles him. Dirt and dust swirl violently as his horse neighs loudly. He covers his face to protect himself from debris. Slowly heading his way is that strange cloud that has grown immense and become dark and malevolent. The cloud begins to change form, taking on the visage of a horrific face, black and cruel, that rushes toward him and says in a thundering voice "Perish, die! Leave this region for it is ours, and we shall not be supplanted. We shall not surrender these souls to Him. They belong to us!"

Strong winds assail the lone prophet and his horse, trying to knock them off the plateau. Feneer holds on to the rocks for dear life. He pulls the staff from his sash and cries out to the Lord. Then his staff begins to crackle with energy, and he slowly resists the power of the wind. The cloud starts to be pushed back, and Feneer sensed that enemy was preparing for a final attack. There was a loud clap of thunder, and heavy rain and hail started pounding him.

So the prophet shouts, "The Lord, my light and shield" and raises his staff against the storm that beats upon him. Rocks crash around him from above as he tries to escape with his horse, leading it down the path. Then anger rises within him, and with his staff raised, a shield of light surrounds him and his horse. The cloud's face becomes enraged. Lightning bolts thunder upon the prophet that burn and sever the rock, causing an avalanche, but the shield protects Feneer and his red steed.

The cloud senses that its attack has failed. It begins to grow blacker until it changes form into a tornado, descending upon Feneer. He lifts his staff, calling for Tempest, sword of power. Lightning from Tempest strikes the tornado, driving it back, its thunderbolts bounce off the shield of light surrounding him and his horse.

Feneer looks up, waving Tempest back and forth as clouds form twisters atop of the evil storm. That made it begin to dissipate. The tornado struggles to hold its form, but lightning and stronger winds causes it to be pulled up. It lets out a roar of agony, breaking apart. All quickly goes silent and still.

Soaked in water and his ears ringing from the sound of thunder, the prophet collapses to the ground. Alongside him, his steed lay, both spent from their ordeal. Surrounding them are debris and craters burned into the hillside from the lightning strikes made by the cloud of evil.

Tired, wet, and alone, Feneer lays silently. His robe and all belongings are soaked, and he begins to cough up water. Then he falls into a deep sleep where a dream overtakes him. After he was rested, he awakens to the beating of the hot sun. The prophet knows not how long he was asleep, but he is strengthened. He looks over to see his horse licking its hoof as if ready to move on.

"I see you are well rested, my friend," said Feneer, wringing out his cloak and the rest of his belongings petting his horse, which he named Bayard for its reddish-brown color.

Then he takes his extra cloak, dries Bayard off, and thanks the Lord for sustaining them in battle. His ribs hurt from being tossed about, his head from the hail and sounds of thunder the cloud brought upon him, but otherwise, he is okay. Mounting his horse, he strides down the mountain with new purpose, wondering what the dream he had truly meant.

Meanwhile the soldiers of Chidarra travel swiftly through the forest until they reach a great lake. It is quiet and calm, with dark murky water and lush vegetation that sprouts from the deep lake bed.

"Strange, I did not know a lake was in these parts," said Luic.

"Do you know of this place, little ones?" asked Endrr.

"No," said Ivan as he leapt off his horse, walking over to Endrr. "I have never even heard of a lake being in these parts, neither from kin nor from wayfarers passing through. It seemed to come out of nowhere."

"Well, this place looks comely enough," said Luic.

Then Endrr turns to the captain, asking, "Do you see where the lake ends and begins, where we may cross or go around? It looks to go on without end."

"I can't tell either. Do any of you know of another way to the homeland of your kinfolk? For I have promised the prophet I would deliver you safe and secure, and we are men of our word," said Luic.

"Of a truth, we ourselves have never been here before, even as messengers for our people. We have never ventured this way or far north, nor have we ever been to the villages of our kinfolk before," said Barran. "All we know is that our kind dwell north in the mountains of Imsdarr."

"Strange, for such a vast lake, there seems to be no sign of animals here, not even a bird—nothing," said Luic.

"Still there seems to be no avoiding its presence unless we look for a route going around it, and who knows how long that may take," said Endrr.

Luic commands two scouts to go in opposite directions, looking for what may be a manageable depth where they may cross the lake. After a period of time, one of the scouts returns with news of a bridge he spotted ahead that they can cross where the lake narrows. Luic sends another soldier to bring back the other scout and to meet them at the bridge.

The other scout dismounts from his horse to walk upon the sandy muddy shoreline. Waves of water and white foam lick the rocks that surround the shore of the lake. The sky is bright blue, with plenty of sunshine that sparkles off the waters. The lake vegetation can be seen floating on top of the dark, quiet, and murky water. Trees surround the huge lake, but still no life can be seen. No fish leaped from the waters, no animals lap it to drink—nothing. The scout grabs a stone, flings it, skipping it upon the water, and begins to walk back when a splash is heard from the lake.

He turns around to see what it is, covering his forehead with his hand for better vision, when his fellow comes and orders his return.

"There is something in these waters," says the scout.

"Maybe so, but we are ordered to meet the band promptly. A bridge has been found where we can cross and be gone from this lonely place," said the other scout.

"Aye, let us be gone then, but keep a close eye out for anything strange, especially in the waters, for who knows what may lurk in it."

His friend laughs and tells him he worries too much, and they both stride away, reaching the others at the bridge.

The bridge is made of stone covered in lush green moss. It is long and wavy, flowing up and down at five peaks, bending slightly crooked from side to side. When the two scouts arrive at the bridge, they see the troop waiting for them. The scout rides up to Luic and tells him that something may be a stir in the waters and to take caution. An insect buzzes around and bites one of the men on the neck. The soldier slapped it off when his fellow smirked at him, shaking his head when he too was bitten.

At the entrance of the bridge was an old oval marble plaque covered in dirt, with words in an unknown language. Endrr walked over to wipe it and asked if the Ciqala could interpret it, but none could. Suddenly the words swirled around, becoming clear to Endrr.

"I don't understand. The words, they-they are made clear to me," said Endrr, astonished. "I can read the saying completely."

"How so?" asked his captain.

"Perhaps an enchantment," said a soldier.

"Read on." Luic gestures.

"Welcome to Serpentine, bridge and the abode of Acionna, the Lady of Aluhr Lake. May all who partake of its path be blessed and may riches and refreshing bring rest to thy eternal soul," read Endrr.

The soldiers look relieved and ask their captain if they may continue their journey when a beautiful woman with long wavy black hair and a see-through blue silk garment wrapped around her curvy form appears on the bridge. Flowers are arrayed in her hair and bracelets of gold adorn her ankles and wrists. Her eyes are bright, with long lashes, and her nails painted red. An amulet made of bluish-green crystal hangs on a chain of flowing, sparkling water circling her neck. All are stunned and overtaken by her beauty. Slowly she strides toward the men, with her bare feet walking overtop the mossy stone walkway.

"Ho there, good fellows. You seek to enter my bridge to hasten your journey north, do you not?" asked the comely woman.

"Indeed we do, most beautiful lady of the lake," said Luic. "Please forgive our intrusion, for we meant no harm."

The woman smiled and assured them, saying, "There is no offense or malice here, my friends, only the welcoming arms of peace and friendship. Look about you."

The men look around to see butterflies of dazzling colors and birds of all sorts singing and flitting about. Fish leaped from glistening waters, with people swimming and welcoming the visitors with songs of delight. Little people wearing strange pointed hats appeared from the woods, dancing and playing instruments in celebration, offering ale to drink that most of the men and Ciqala eagerly partook of.

"Welcome, friends, to the home of Acionna, the Lady of the Ahlur and friend of the weary," said a little man, piping and dancing about. "May she bless you and keep you on your path."

"Pardon me, but what are you called? For we've never seen your kind before," asked Faolan.

"We are lake gnomes," responded a little woman, smiling and prancing about.

Then Acionna walked over to Luic, putting a necklace of solid flowing water around his neck, relaxing him. A rainbow of colors appeared over the bridge on each side of the waters that awed the senses. Across the rainbow, friendly men and beautiful women waved excitedly, welcoming them to their home in the lake. They become mad with desire for these beauties across the bridge and for the alluring damsels swimming in the waters.

The Ciqala were smitten with gnome women that danced with them and whispered in their ears, making their hearts merry with wine. For the little ones still had heavy hearts because of the dirge of death that laid waste to their village and kinfolk. Luic approached Acionna on one knee and told her how incredibly beautiful she was and took her hand in his as he was about to kiss it. Suddenly a loud howl was heard in the distance, alerting everyone to look in that direction. The great black wolf could be seen running toward them.

The wolf circled the troop, sniffing and growling at the gnomes, then approached the water, snarling at the people. Birds and butterflies flew around it, and the wolf backed away, digging its paws in the grass, churning up dirt. Then it walked past the men and slowly onto the bridge, where Luic was transfixed at the beauty of the lady of the lake, Ahlur. The wolf growled deeply as its eyes turned bloodred. Foam began to froth from its fanged mouth. Luic turned around to look at the wolf, staring at the queen, still holding her hand when he asks, "What is it, wolf? Be still for we are among friends."

Then the wolf lunges at the queen, who backs away, clutching on to the hand of Luic, holding him in front of her for protection.

Faolan cries out, "God of Feneer, Captain, behind you!"

Luic looks at the hand he was holding to find it dark green, clawed, and dripping with slime. He turns to see a horrible she creature with rotten lake weed for hair. It had fangs and glowing eyes made of dirty water that flowed down her putrid form. Crabs and eels crept through her mud-laden body, and her amulet was not crystal at all but a misshapen skull, its necklace not flowing water but a poisonous serpent that clung to her neck, hissing.

Luic was quickly backing away, frightened, when his sparkling necklace became a serpent, squeezing his throat. His men's spell broken, they frantically aided Luic, removing the snake, which evaporated. Weapons were raised for battle when the gnomes turned into little evil, mocking, grotesque creatures that stood back, awaiting their queen's orders. The wolf jumped between Luic and Acionna, growling and standing its ground. Endrr looked across the lake to see the gruesome forms of their would-be friends salivating, awaiting them on the other side of the now slimy bridge.

"The Lord has sent the wolf to break the enchantment of the monster," said Luic, "else we all would have been . . ."

"Devoured in the gullets of my servants, fool," laughed Acionna. "You humans are so easily tricked and led astray, not by sorcery but by the lust of your own hearts and the corruption of your sinful minds."

"Liar," shouted Endrr, "it was your enchantment that—"

"That showed you what you wanted to see. The illusion was only brought on by what was in your own soul, son of Adam. And just as he was deceived by the serpent, so have you been fooled, and to your own ruin," mocked the ancient creature. "Look about you and despair, for none can deliver you from my hands."

Then the grass turned gray and the ground moldy. The trees around the lake began to die and lose their leaves, swaying back and forth as an eerie wind began to howl. The sun lost its shine, and the people in the waters turned into monsters that sang a hellish song that began to bewitch the men into surrender. However, the wolf was not affected by the enchantment, attacking Acionna and her gnomes, howling loudly and breaking the spell from off the men.

This angered the queen, who summoned evil biting and stinging dragonflies from the lake to attack the men, causing confusion among the ranks. Then she called for her dark gnomes to attack by clawing and biting the soldiers, who fought back, slaying several of the creatures. The Ciqala brandished their daggers and leaped around, darting to and fro, stabbing the gnomes, aiding their comrades. The queen began to approach when again the wolf met her, not allowing her to pass from off the bridge when her rage was kindled against it. Luic saw what was happening, took from his belt three round blades in each hand, and threw them at the demon queen.

She laughed as they went through her murky mud form without harm, and then she called for the creatures in the lake to destroy the band that fought valiantly. When suddenly the wolf howled greatly to the heavens, and the darkened sky broke with light that seared the creatures surrounding the soldiers, keeping them at bay and causing many to flee back to the depths and dead timber. Those across the bridge screamed in despair as flames engulfed them from beneath the earth that opened, swallowing them alive as their smoke rose high in the air.

Acionna looked up in terror but stood firm, causing the dead grass to grow and hold the men and their horses in place so they could not flee. As she ran with claws raised to slay them, the light struck her and burned her sore. Her screams shook the lake as she writhed in agony, trying to flee to its waters for safety. She could not, for the Lord had judged her and counted her rule of that region broken this day. The light surrounded her, caused her murky form to catch fire, drying out, and just as she was about to enter the water, she cracked, screamed, and broke apart, falling into dust. The Lord caused His light to soak the entire lake, even down to its bottom, destroying the monstrous creatures that hid in secret and banishing ancient spirits that held sway in the deep, making way for natural life to return.

The trees that were all but dead returned to life, and the spirits that afflicted them were banished from that place, causing branches to grow and leaves to sprout. Singing was heard as the creation sang a song unto the Lord for freeing it from the curse that was placed upon it, albeit the curse of Adam still held its place and would return after the appointed time until its short suspension lifts. Then it will regain its foothold until the great day of deliverance.

The grass that was dead and held them in place became lush and green again as flowers of various sorts sprouted forth, with butterflies dancing around them. Birds and bees flew overhead and went from flower to flower. The splash of water could be heard as ducks and swan made themselves at home in the lake. Frogs sang their songs and fish leaped from the water, which turned crystal clear where you could see the bottom.

The men looked in awe and could not believe their eyes. They looked at each other with mouths open. Taking off their garments, they jumped in the water, shouting for joy. The horses pranced, following them in, and drank the clean water, filling their bellies, quenching their thirst. The sun was hot, but the water was cool. Then beavers, foxes, and several bear rambled forth, enjoying the water, not attacking one another. It was as if the whole lake and everything in it turned into a beautiful paradise that all men long for. The Ciqala ran to and fro, singing and dancing, forgetting all about the loss of their village and loved ones, if only for a moment. Wounds begin to heal on the soldiers, and clarity of mind and spirit refresh all.

Their sight became keener; they could see longer distances and focus on the smallest things. Colors became brighter, and they could hear things from afar. It seemed as if they were close to them. Even their sense of smell was changed, for the scents around them sprang forth as a lush garden filled with various kinds of plants and fruits. This went on for the span of about an hour.

A woman, or what seemed to be a woman shrouded in light and robed in white, appeared before them. The light cloaked her face, so she could not be seen as she stood in the lush green grass on the bank of the lake.

A fox and an Argonian leopard walked up to her. She petted them on their backs. Soon birds and insects gently flew over her head until the soldiers and Ciqala ramble forth out of the water to approach the glowing being before them.

"Hail men of Chidarra and Ciqala of Abbonwood," said the woman.

Then the soldiers and their tiny allies stood before her, half robed and wet. They bowed their heads when Luic stepped forth and went to one knee, showing respect. "Hail to you, milady. You know of us, but to whom are we so honored to speak to?"

With those words, the woman walks toward Luic as the animals make a path for her. A squirrel leaps off the back of a fox and runs up to him, jumping on his outstretched hand, scurrying up his arm and resting on his shoulder, tickling him as the woman speaks in a calm and soothing voice. "This place is beautiful, is it not?" she asks.

"Very beautiful," responds Luic. Then the glowing figure takes him by the hand and raises him up as he covers his eyes to shield them from the light.

Calmly she walks over to the five tiny ones and bends over, looking upon them. The Ciqala smile and reach for her hands and begin to dance with her and sing joyful songs while the soldiers look on, smiling. Then she stops her dancing and departs, walking toward the soldiers, who look on quietly.

"Come close to me," she says as the soldiers surround her, some of them with tears in their eyes that roll down their cheeks.

"Listen well and heed my words for I was sent from the Lord God who has given you victory over your enemies. The Lord loves you very, very much."

As those words were spoken, the men from the greatest to the least began to well up. Some of them even began to sob. Some fell to their knees while others stood, trying to hold back emotions that welled deep from within. However, they could not, for the more they tried, the more they cried, as if a well of water gushed and spilled over. Then they wiped their eyes and gathered themselves as she looked on, comforting them.

"I feel comfort but am overwhelmed with shame for my heart is wicked," said a soldier while another said, "How could any love me for I am an abuser of maids who seduces and robs them of their purity?"

Yet another states, "My own father and mother abandoned me when I was a child and left me alone in this world. I have never known love, but hate and sadness ever ruled my spirit, and yet with those mere words alone, I feel for the first time a love and acceptance that I have never known."

"The Lord chose you to see this place that was ruled by Acionna, a dark and dreadful power who lured and destroyed many souls in this region since the fall of Itvihiland. He did this so that you may not only witness his power but also his love and compassion. Far too long, evil ruled these lands to the desolation of all, but God delivered her into your hands. Her time has ended," said the woman.

"But God has heard the cries of the innocent and those who seek peace and refuge from their tormentors, and He has chosen you to be His hammer against the cruel masters of these lands, to remove their influence forever. But he will not force you. The choice must be yours," she said.

And to a man, they pressed their hands against their breasts and bowed their heads and said, "We will do as the Lord God commands this day forward and bring peace to the land."

Then the woman glowed bright and prayed, saying, "Lord God you have heard with their own mouths these men You have chosen to follow You and bring judgment to those who pillage the helpless and rule with merciless hate. Give them wisdom and understanding, teaching them Your ways of compassion and righteousness to those in need. Let them not abuse their power or authority You have given them but guide them by Your word and strong hand. Let Your angels watch over them and keep them from harm, showing them good from evil. El-Elyon, let them call upon Your name, and You will hear and answer them, for You are their strong tower and help in times of trouble. As You prospered and delivered David, son of Jesse, so do to these."

Then she turns to Luic and lays hands upon his head, saying, "You were chosen by God to be the head and not the tail and be a mighty warrior for the Lord of Hosts. Rule your men with compassion and confidence in the Lord and not of yourself, for your victory comes from above. Give honor unto those whom honor is due and be humble and not prideful, for if pride enters your heart, your fall and destruction will be great, and you will be given over to your enemies, for to whom much is given, much is required. Elohim is indeed with you, Luic, son of Alphor, and His mercy endures forever. Remember this as you judge and rule over others great and small."

Turning her attention to Endrr, she says, "Endrr, son of Vera, you are a wise lion among men. Your heart is true to your captain and his men for you would give your life for them. Truly, you are a brave and strong warrior before the Lord, and His hand is with you to guide and keep you. Fear not those who seek evil or harm to you and bend your knees in prayer before His face often for this shall be your truest aid and weapon against those bent on your destruction."

Finally, she turns toward the little ones and smiles greatly, though they cannot see it. She kneels down and calls them closer. Then she hugs them and they her as she says, "All that is left of Abbonwood, five souls in all. You who are most precious to the Lord, not because you are greatest but rather least among us, for you have suffered greatly, my friends. The two messengers, Ivan and Barran, swift as the east winds and ever present to run an errand for your former king Arno, who you served faithfully. God has seen your faithfulness and courage and shall esteem you in high regard in due time."

Then she turns to Faolan, Egan, and Goban and declares, "You three friends are inseparable and love one another greatly. Truly a three-cord band not easily broken and tender in the heart of the Lord. Faolan, son of Cerin, Egan, son of Honer, and Goban, son of Garsam, your hearts know peace here, and yet I sense your thoughts drift elsewhere."

The three friends look at one another when Goban says, "Our thoughts are towards our friend Feneer, the prophet we met back at Abbonwood who set us all on this journey to the land of Imsdarr and Junayd, the mountain village of our kinfolk.

"For some reason, we cannot take our minds off of him," said Faolan. After hearing those words, the woman says, "Indeed your mind is bent on your friend for it is the Lord's will to send you to him for He needs you."

"He needs us," the three say in astonishment.

"Powerful and wise he is, but still he's in need of companions. Feneer goes against great foes, and often alone, he travels helping those in need while proclaiming the goodness of the Lord. Many times he has faced death and seen horrors that most men would perish at just the sight of. His heart is heavy and shoulders weary, little ones, and if you would know the truth, he misses you greatly and thinks of you often."

"Milady, send us to him, we ask you, for if there is any way we could help him, we will," said Egan.

The three Ciqala beg her to send them to him, declaring that even if they are little help to him, they don't want him to be alone. With that request, she prays unto the Lord, asking him if their request could be granted, and then turns her attention to Luic and says, "Captain, you are to return to Chidarra at once and await the coming of the prophet.

"Should he delay long, instructions shall be sent to you, but tell no one of what you have seen and heard, not even of your battles, nor of your allegiance to the Lord, do you understand?" she says firmly.

"I do," said Luic, "but what of the little ones? The prophet commanded me to deliver them to their kinfolk, and I swore to do so."

"You are to follow the word of the Lord. The two messengers shall stay with me while you venture back, for the Lord has plans for them," she said.

"And what of us, milady? Our friend needs us, and though we would remain in this oasis, our hearts are with him," said Goban, bowing before her.

"Please, we beg you," cried Faolan.

Then the lady in white raised her hands high and shouted, "Oh Lord God, you have heard their request. They seek to be of aid to your servant Feneer. Shall they stay here, go with the band back to their kingdom, or go to the prophet. What say you, All-Knowing One?"

Then three large male deer with huge antlers walked up to the three, and after that, three huge hawks the likes of which had not been seen glide down on the other side of them. They towered over the little ones and spread their wings in unison. Then three great bears walked behind them and nudged their backs with their snouts to get their attention. When they saw them, the bears stood high on their hind legs, displaying their size and strength before gently sitting beside them.

"The Lord has heard your request and granted it. You are to choose your method of transportation from these you see before you: The great fire hawks of the land of Orar, who fear nothing and have even aided in the ancient battles of King Thaes against the dragons of Laurogor. The giant bears of Kodu, who make way for no one and can travel great distances. Their power is in their jaws and claws, and they are not to be trifled with. You will have no problem with them by your side. Finally, the deer of Avalla. Quiet as they are swift and powerful, able to leap great distances and hide, not being seen by the keenest of eyes. Their senses are sharp, and they are a friend to those friendly to them but a fierce adversary to those of ill intent. Now, thus says the Lord, choose your mode of travel."

The three friends look intently at the beasts the Lord brought before them and huddle together, conversing with one another.

Then Egan gently walks to the fire hawks as they look upon him with eyes that pierce his soul. He notices just how much they tower over him, about the span of two full-grown men, with their sharp massive talons that could carry a small cow and have been known to rip through dragon's scales. Their color is reddish gold, and the crest around their neck is snow white, as are the feathers upon their legs. With wings that block out the sun and feathers soft and beautiful, one could just imagine flying with these great beasts.

Egan walks back, nodding his head to Goban as the Ciqala turns and faces the great bears of Kodu. Huge and daunting for the eyes to behold, truly a fearful sight for men and beasts to encounter, they look as if there is more going on in their souls than meets the eyes.

"You would only need one of them to take all three of us," Goban says to himself as he touches the bear's claws, which are sharp to the touch. Thick burly brown fur encases a muscular frame, with strong jaws and teeth that protrude on each side that they use for crushing the bones of prey much larger than themselves. Leaves gently fall overhead to the ground as a faint breeze flows through the lake.

Egan takes a step back when Faolan gently walks toward the deer of Avalla. These deer are large and powerful yet sleek and swift looking. With antlers that crown their heads that would put any king's crown to shame, they seem almost regal themselves. They have long powerful legs and sturdy hooves used to not only travel thick brush in the forest but also to climb mountainous terrain like the mountain goats of Imsdarr.

As Faolan continues to pet one of them, he notices its coat begin to change color to mimic the shade of his attire, and Faolan says, "Amazing," out loud as everyone else looks on. Then he quietly turns and returns to his friends as they huddle and debate the choice they should make. Finally they walk close to the maiden in shining apparel. Faolan says, "Milady, we choose the deer of Avalla for our journey."

She raised her hands and said, "A wise choice, my little friends" as she glides past them with a train of light flowing behind her to the bridge that was once moss-covered stone but has now become a beautiful gold with a bright crystal walkway. Two columns of marble mixed with fire are raised high above it on each side with a beautiful rainbow archway.

Upon the rainbow archway are words written in blue and scarlet flame that say "Eye has not seen, nor ear heard, nor has it entered into the heart of man what God has prepared for those that love Him."

Upon the columns of stone and fire were precious gems and jewels of all sorts that sparkled in blinding brilliance as tongues of flame dance about them through the stone.

At seeing this, men held their mouths and shook their heads, unable to comprehend the beauty before them. Endrr extends his hand, touching a column when he feels a soothing sensation as the men show respect to God. Indeed, everything there seems to emanate a holy reverence and tranquility.

Then the lady says, "This is a haven for the weary, destitute, and those who seek hope, the presence of the Lord. It is a gift to those who would believe in Adonai, repent, and turn to righteousness, showing kindness to their fellow man. It is but a dim shadow of what He shall restore after all sin is purged from the earth—no, all creation throughout the cosmos. The gentile nations shall truly know that He indeed is, as do the children of Israel, His chosen. For by the seed of Abraham are all nations blessed to know the Word of the Living God."

Then she walks underneath the archway and says, "This shall be called El Aman Cether, which means 'Faithful God, My Hiding Place,' and thus shall many who seek Him find its path, even the unworthy, for his grace falls on them as well. God takes no pleasure in seeing anyone damned. But to the evil and cruel and those with malice in their hearts, this place shall be unseen invisible and unattainable. It is God's wish for those who visit here to find refreshment, gaining knowledge of His care for all men, but most of all, to experience the loving touch and visitation of God, our Redeemer, the King of Grace. But it lasts only for short a season in time as testament of His faithfulness."

A soldier walks over to the woman and asks, "Can we stay, milady, for who would want to leave such a place as this? The longer we tarry, the more beautiful it becomes. Milady, this is what all men long for in their hearts."

"Didn't you promise to serve the Lord? Seek more the creator of this haven and less the haven itself, for in Him lies true rest, even in the darkest most trying of times," says the woman.

Then she turns to Ivan and Barran. "Stand by my side for you are to stay with me. You three, come quickly for I must pray for you on your journey."

Prayer flows from deep within her as a crystal vial of oil appears in her hands, and she anoints the three Ciqala for their journey. The oil is thick and golden, with a sweet smell, as it runs from the top of their heads all the way down their faces while they kneel with their heads bowed. Faolan spreads his arms out and asks for a double portion, and so his request is granted, and she pours the vial of golden oil upon him again. As he is covered in oil, he begins to sweat greatly and to feel as if he is on fire.

With his eyes closed, he shouts, "I feel as if I am on fire from within and without, but it does not burn. It is a strange sensation."

"The power of God flows upon you, my son," she says. "Now wipe your eyes but allow the oil to stay. It shall remove itself soon enough. Quickly, grab your belongings and get atop your deer, for your friend will need you soon enough."

The comrades grab their sacks and climb atop their kneeling deer as the lady says, "Now walk across the bridge of Ori and go through the doors of purity and fear not the flames that they are made of for you are worthy to pass through.

"There you shall see two great keepers of El Amon Cether armed for battle from head to toe with flaming swords and shields. They are exceedingly fierce for the Lord has sent them as guardians to protect the entrance of the safe haven. Fear them not, but do not provoke them, and as you pass, you shall come to a cobblestoned road made of gems and smooth pearls, with beautiful trees lined on each side of it. This will take you to a large weeping willow called Goral in the middle that parts the road into two sides. If the tree opens a doorway in its middle, take it, and if not, take the right side of the road, and you will be on the path you need to go."

Then she points them on their way and says, "Be strong and be of good courage for the Lord your God is with you. Trust in Him, and He shall direct your paths."

The three pass by the soldiers when Luic says, "Take care, my friends. The prophet is counting on you. Until we meet again then?"

The Ciqala nod their heads and ride over the bridge made of gold and crystal that shimmers a rainbow of colors with each step. Many symbols creatures and beings of earthen and unearthly origin adorn its gold railings.

"Look, it's those winged creatures on the staff of Feneer carved into the railway," said Faolan.

"Not only that, look at the picture of a great figure on a throne with beings of light all around it. Could that be the Lord?" asked Goban.

"Look we have come to the end and the flaming doors of purity. So shall we now pass from paradise back to a world full of sorrow," sighed Egan.

They pass through the large flaming doors that give great heat but do not burn them until they reach the outside where they see the road made of gems and pearls. On each side of the entrance stand the two enormous warriors the lady spoke of. They are at least twenty-four feet tall and wreathed in bronze flame. Their faces are covered in fierce-looking helmets, their armor is thick from head to toe, with shields and swords made of a blazing white-hot unknown metal. They said not a word, nor did they move, but stood silently guarding the entrance. Goban waved to one of them to try to get their attention when Egan nudged for him to stop it until they reached a different area. There they saw a heavy canopy of mist hovering above trees of different kinds with many fruits to choose from on each side of the path as far as the eyes could see.

One of the trees gently knelt its branches over to them along the walkway, showing them its luscious ripe green fruit.

"Did you see that, Goban?" said Egan. "I think it wants us to pick and eat its fruit."

"Look, another on the other side is doing the same thing," said Faolan.

The Ciqala look behind them to see if the giant guards are watching them, uncertain of their response, when a voice is heard saying, "Pick and eat."

The three look around at each other to see where the voice is coming from, but no one is seen. The voice again says, "Pick of the fruit and eat, for it will give you strength on your journey, but you must eat it here for it will disappear once you leave the garden."

"Dear sir, we beg your pardon, but may we ask who is speaking to us?" asked Faolan.

"I AM," the voice said softly. "Now take and eat for the tree desires for you to taste its fruit. It's quite tasty, you know."

Looking at one another, Goban and Egan grab a piece of the oblong red fruit and bit into it. As the juice runs down their cheeks, their bodies feel strengthened.

"This is *sooo* good," they both say at the same time as they eat of its meat. Faolan runs across to another tree whose branches are lowered for him to taste of its fruit.

The tree drops a round fruit that is gold on one side and blue on the other into his hand. He looks at it and begins to eat it when he also feels refreshed. The scent of the fruit is as good as the fruit itself as he bites into it more and more. Blue and gold nectar gush all over his face as his friends laugh at him and he laughs at himself. Then the voice said, "Do you like the fruit, little ones?"

"Yes, indeed we do, good sir, uh, Mr. I AM, sir," said Goban shyly. "May we please take a few on our way because they are so delicious and tasty, if you don't mind?"

A still quiet takes hold of the place, and when no answer is given, they wonder if that was a question best left unasked until laughter is heard and I Am speaks. "Okay, I will allow it. You may pick five fruits from any of the trees you see but remember, only five. Do not eat them right away. Save them for yourselves when you are hungry, thirsty, or weary on your journey as they will refresh you in times of lack. Eat of them only when needed, for they will remain fresh and not rot."

Dismounting, they run into the garden of trees and flowers that line the walkway on each side, looking at all the fruit that is pleasant to the eyes as the chirping of lovely birds known and unknown fills the air.

They laugh and climb the trees, feeling at home in this beautiful wood that reminds them that they are truly tree folk. Swiftly they climb and dart about with balance and grace, laughing and playing in the trees as they look at all the fruit plants, vines, bushes, and tender foliage, running through the beautiful green grass. It was an orchard of stunning gourds, flowers, and greenery as far as the eye can see. Vegetables and plants of many beautiful shapes, some very odd and extremely unusual while some uniform in nature paint the diverse landscape. Others were so small the petals could barely be seen, but their fragrance was exhilarating, and some were so great in size and scope they towered among the trees themselves with thick leaves of all colors and branches that spread out in all directions.

The sights smells and feel of this place satiates the senses to the full. Then they noticed fantastic insects with differing forms and sizes dancing to and from plant to plant sucking their sweet, syrupy nectar. Some of the insects looked frightening, with large bodies and long wings, many legs, and sharp stingers while others were less daunting but were beautiful and colorful. They seemed to crawl or fly around the young trio.

There were birds, reptiles, cattle, monkeys, and animals small and great, known and never before seen that existed in harmony, feeding upon the lovely ripe fruit dangling from the rich vegetation deeper in the land of wonder that is similar but different from the place they left behind. They were so caught up in the moment, looking at the different kinds of grass, large unique rock formations, waterways, far-off snow-covered mountain ranges, and creatures surrounding them that they walked around, losing themselves in the land of wonder that seems to have no end. The sun was even bigger and brighter here than usual, giving of its life sustaining warmth

It was Faolan that snapped out of the astonishment and told them they had to choose their fruit and be gone, not wanting to lose precious time. They choose their five fruits, each of different sizes, colors, and textures and fly back to the deer, which look strangely at them.

"What is it?" asked Goban. "They look as if something is wrong."

"They want you to share your fruit with them. Now pick one each so they may taste and eat also," said I Am.

"Oh, okay, sorry for our rudeness, friends, we will be right back," said Egan, petting his deer.

Then a green-and-white tree with long, thick, blue leafy vines up in the distance is seen shaking its leaves and dropping fruit on the road, so they mount and ride until they reach it, and the deer take and eat of it, and afterward they burp loudly, and the Ciqala giggle to themselves. They ride until reaching the great weeping willow parting the road. It is tall and wide, with a broad crown of sparkling lush, thick hanging branches that produce a shimmering silvery brilliance. A wind passes through its long green leaves, causing the tree to sway and sing a melodic song that courses through the body, bringing ease and delight to the soul.

They look on transfixed and slowly dismount, gently rubbing the tree that sways rhythmically before them, and after the tree doesn't open, they take the road to the right where overhead, it becomes dark as night. Stars shine in clusters of unimaginable colors and radiance, illuminating their path.

"Planets, suns, and moons all around us and things indescribable that no eyes ever beheld. What is this place?" asked Faolan. "It's like we're walking through the heavens themselves."

The little ones reach out their hands to touch the celestial objects all around them that seem alive and so near but are so far when a bright star in front of them opens, revealing a forest with a dirt path. Slowly they march through the gateway, looking to a strange region they have never seen.

Back at the El Amon, Cether, the maiden of the Lord, tells Luic to be strong and brave and rule his men as he has with mercy and goodness. Moreover, she bade him o remember to tell no one of what was seen or heard until the time appointed when the prophet would meet him in Chidarra. If there is a great delay, instructions would be given as to what he is to do. Then the black wolf walks and sits by his side as he says, "He has been a great friend and ally to us. I am very fond of this wolf."

"His name is Nuntis, and he left his pack to stay with you," she said. "A gift from above, no doubt. Now go and follow the path as spoken to you. Fear not the guardians, but do not tempt them. When you get to the path, take the left road, and you shall be where you need to go."

"Hide the two clubs that you took for spoil, safe from any eyes until they are needed to confirm your journey to your king and those in authority. Now go, and may the Lord be with you."

"What is your name, so we may tell others of your kindness, milady?" asks Endrr.

"A servant of the Lord," she responds mysteriously. "When the time comes, tell others about His kindness, and you shall do well."

Slowly Luic and his men, along with Nuntis, pass on, saying good-bye to her, Ivan, and Barran until they cross the bridge and pass through the fires of purity and on their journey back to Chidarra, leaving behind the paradise that deep in their hearts they wish they didn't have to depart. Onward they go, passing the guardians, avoiding eye contact so not to offend them, until they enter the walkway full of beautiful trees, flowers, and animals that cause them to stop and stare in wonder. Finally, they gaze upon the great weeping willow. They were marveling at its size and splendor as it towered over them when a voice utters softly, "Be strong and know that I Am with you, never leaving nor forsaking you."

The men look around to see where the voice is coming from but feel its love and authority coursing through their being, as if the words themselves were alive and full of power. Luic looked up and, in reverence, thanked the voice for its favor and kind words, fearing to ask if they had heard the voice of Almighty God Himself! Heeding the weeping willow's directions, they took the left path and entered the realm of stars, where everyone gasps. A stir of amazement takes their collective breaths away. Then Endrr can no longer hold back and says, "This truly is beyond belief. How much more can the mind and the senses take before one loses them?"

They see stars forming and sunbursts of heat and light. Moons and planets of gigantic proportions, and many small, are swirling about in a perfect order, standing in the black void of nothingness. Strange sounds and colorful beams of lights emanate from pulsating clusters of enigmatic celestial bodies that seem to harmonize as though they were living things. Then ahead of them, the blackness slowly forms a doorway where they reluctantly walk through, hardly believing the beauty and wonder that their eyes have just witnessed.

FIVE

RUN, RUN FROM THE MOON, THY ENEMY

The soldiers trek through ways that seemed lightly traveled, with Nuntis close beside until they come to a fork in the road. There were two paths. One seemed pleasant, sporting lush trees to cover them from the heat of the sun, with a mossy, fern-covered ground. Mulberry trees and bushes with evergreen, birch, hackberry, and maple trees litter the more pleasant path. The other less comfortable way was mud laden from a small creek, with insects and a sparse tree line where they would have no relief from the heat of the day.

Luic asked Endrr which path to take. Nuntis went ahead and sniffed both roads. His response was a curious one for he sniffed the less appealing path as if it were generous to them while the fruitful path he shunned. After seeing this, Endrr thought maybe it would be wise to follow that which seemed desolate rather than the other, but the men adjured the captain to take the former for it was pleasant to the eyes and covered them from sun and rain. In addition, it was better to lodge at night under the shade of trees rather than an open field, and with that thought Luic took the goodly path, and the men were appeased.

On they slowly went on horseback, not knowing where they were but trusting in the word given them by the woman of light who said they would find their way. The path had many fruitful vines that hung from the trees with flowers that smelled refreshing and the various sounds of the wild all around them. The cool of the air was much better than the heat of the sun on their backs and necks, for sure. They picked boysenberries and mulberries, enjoying the scenery. Still did Nuntis seem more and more uneasy about their surroundings, a fact that did not go unnoticed by Endrr, more so than Luic.

Soon they came upon a high wall of rock to the right of them with a slight flow of water running down its side. Strange markings like scratches were cut deep into the rock. The men looked but said nothing and kept their trek until they reached open land with tall grass in the cool of the day. It is there on a hillside they decide to rest.

"Ahh, what a sight this is," said Luic to Endrr. "How are the men and their provisions?"

"All is well, Captain, but I still don't know where we are or where we should be headed. I have never seen this land before, and neither have any of the other men. Scenic as it is, your wolf seems not to like it much," said Endrr, watching Nuntis pace back and forth uneasily.

Luic acknowledges this, then takes out a lens rolled in copper to search the land. In the distance, beyond the hills and trees, he sees smoke rising in the sky. Then he runs to a higher hill for a better look, but he still can't tell the smoke's origin.

"What is it, what do you see?" asked Endrr.

"See for yourself," said Luic. "Perhaps there is a friendly village where we can find lodging for the night instead of here or in the patch of timber up ahead."

"Agreed," said Endrr. "I will gather the men, and we should be there before the dead of nightfall."

Endrr gathered the men, and on they went, up and down grassy slopes until they reached the wooded area. There they galloped swiftly trough the horse-ridden path as the night descended upon them with a mist that slowly crept upon the forest floor. The men dismounted and lit torches to light their way until they reached a clearing. The outskirts of a town could be seen through the bright moonlight and stars.

The smell of food filled their nostrils, and their stomachs began to yearn, fueling them to walk faster until they reached large black gates where they are met by two gatekeepers and a watchman in a high tower.

"Ho, friends, we be soldiers of the kingdom of Chidarra on a long journey home, and we seek lodgings for the night if possible," said Luic.

"How many be you?" asked a tall stout gatekeeper.

"Forty in all, with horses and our belongings. If it would be no trouble, we seek food also and would be most grateful," said Luic.

The gatekeeper looked at them and called for a sentry inside the gate. Then he sent him with word to the town elders of the situation while much busyness and clamor was heard inside.

The gate was wood covered with thick black pitch. It had a stone wall for support, with spikes of iron and shards of glass turning inward. It was truly dreadful. Soon the sentry came back with word allowing the men to come in for lodging, and the gatekeeper called for the gates to be opened. On the inside, the men saw many people, young and old, singing, dancing, drinking ale, and carrying on by fires. Others looked not at all cheerful but rather somber faced, hardly holding their heads up to be noticed. The sentry escorted them past many huts and homes, large and small. Some were row homes on each side, forming long streets lighted by candles in the windows

Most looked at the soldiers with welcoming faces while others, not so much. Then the sentry took them to mysterious a castle made of black stone with red stained glass windows and guards placed throughout. Waiting was a tall man with a red cape, white shirt, black pants, and red shoes. His hair was dark, thick, and long, and he had a short, trimmed black beard with gray eyes. With him was a very beautiful lady in a white gown, with long curly blonde hair and blue eyes.

"Greetings, men of Chidarra, and welcome to the town of Turnskin. I am Blaeld, and this is Emwet. We are the elders, and we welcome you to our humble abode."

The mood is light and hospitable, with servants beckoning the soldiers to dismount from their horses, leading them away to a pen where they can feed drink and rest. Then other servants appear before Blaeld as he commands them to lead the men to their sleeping quarters. Turnskin is quite large, with people looking out of windows and doors with smiling faces or looks of suspicion. A few look with emptiness, as if without hope, and turn their heads so not to be noticed by the guards.

The soldiers come upon a row of small wooden huts with flat-sloped roofs. Inside is a dirt floor with a small fireplace and two cots for sleeping—modest but it gets the job done. There is one small wooden table and two chairs with an empty pitcher for water and two clay bowls to eat and drink from. The men lodge four to a hut while the servants bring them blankets and well water to fill their pitchers. They are very tired and want to rest their bodies from all the riding and traveling they have endured.

Luic looks upon the mantle of the fireplace and sees oil. A woman enters with a torch, lighting a warm fire for them. Luic was sitting in a chair with his wolf, resting near the flame for heat, when a knock is heard at the door. Luic opens the door to see a meek thin porter standing there looking at him.

"May I come in, sir?" asked the porter as he looks at the wolf, which was staring at him silently by the fire.

"Yes, of course, come in, and thank your lord for the hospitality he have shown myself and my men," responded Luic.

"Indeed, milord," said the porter. "My name is Rothiro, and I shall attend to the needs of you and your men. Blaeld shall summon you when food and provisions are prepared in the morning. If you need anything until then, I will be right outside your door."

"Again thank you for your hospitality, Rothiro, is it?" asked Luic as he notices him looking intently at Nuntis.

"That is a big dire wolf you have there," said Rothiro. "He looks menacing."

"He can be if trifled with. His name is Nuntis," said Luic as he walks over and rubs him behind his ears. Rothiro says nothing and abruptly leaves, quietly closing the door behind him.

Later that night, one of the soldiers awakens from his sleep and, wrapped in his blanket, opens the door, leaving behind his fellows. He notices a guard with a sword by his side standing across the road next to a glowing lamppost, looking at him. Then he turns and notices another standing in the darkness seven huts down, with sword glistening in the moonlight. He walks past him, looking behind. The guard says nothing. He comes to a bush behind one of the huts, where he pulls his pants down and relieves himself.

Afterward he comes back to see the guard still standing stiff as can be. Looking throughout the village, he sees guards placed everywhere out in the open, in secret, upon rooftops and placed in homes seen through the candlelit windows. He passes the guard standing silently going toward his lodgings. He opens the door and hears a slight animalistic snarl. He looks back at the guard, who does not move, and then walks in and closes the door behind him, grabbing his weapons by his side. Quietly he sits upon his cot, looking at his large friend snoring loudly across from him and two others on the floor. An eerie feeling comes over him that he cannot shake.

There he sits until morning, holding his sword in his hand and staring at the wooden door before him. That morning, all the men were awakened by the ringing of bells, festive music, and the loud knocking on their doors by the servants who beckon them to awake themselves for breakfast. They leave their quarters. Most are led to washing huts, where rags, water-filled cauldrons, and soap are brought to them to use for bathing. After this, they are taken to the town center, where rows of tables are prepared for them, with fruits, hard-boiled eggs, bacon, and bread are served with water and milk to drink. The musicians play songs that are comely to the ears as children run about, playing happily and without care.

Then Blaeld and Emwet, followed by six other village elders, came and presented themselves before the men, bidding them to eat and enjoy the festive moment. It was a beautiful sun-filled morning, and the warmth felt good to all. Emwet and Blaeld sat across from Luic and Endrr to make conversation.

"I am so sorry, my friend, for my lack of manners. For last night, I didn't even ask your names," exclaimed Blaeld.

"I am Luic, captain of these men, and this is my commander, Endrr, who is as my brother.

"We hope you find our lodgings acceptable to you and your men, Captain, especially under such short notice," said Emwet.

"Yes, had we known afore time of your coming, better arrangements would have been made, but under the circumstances we did the best we could," said Blaeld.

"All is fine, my friends, most assuredly. We are grateful, but we will trouble you no further for we must be off soon to our homeland," said Luic.

"Oh, we were hoping to have you stay at least a while longer for it is rare our village gets visitors such as yourselves. You are most welcome here," said Emwet, wearing a gold amulet and gaudy pearl earrings. Her fingernails were painted black and her full lips red, with her long curly hair tied in a tight bun. She had white skin and wore a blue and white dress that displayed her curvy form. Her feet were adorned with blue pearl studded sandals.

She looks down to see Nuntis by the side of Luic. The wolf stared at her when she calls for a server to give him food and water, but Nuntis will not eat or drink anything but instead sits alertly by his master's side. The wolf, however, is not alone in his trepidation, for the soldier Wier, who strolled out the night before, will not eat either, to the contempt of those sitting around him.

"Why won't you eat the food?" asked Snourn quietly to Wier, his bunk mate. "It is most rude of you to reject the offering of these people."

"Because you didn't see what I did last night, my friend," said Wier. "Whilst you snored away, I took a stroll to relieve myself, and all around, not just us but as far as the eye could see, were guards placed about."

"Perhaps as a precaution of our presence. We are soldiers, are we not?" asked Snourn. "And as was already spoken by Emwet, they are not used to many travelers, much less soldiers, in these parts."

"True," said Wier, "but have you not noticed how the wolf reacts to this place? He won't even drink or eat of its food. And what of the sad faces mixed with the happy ones? The look in their eyes is one of hopelessness that cannot be openly shown, I tell you."

Snourn shakes his head and continues to eat his food, ignoring his friend. A group of children playing tag run around and underneath the table. Wier begins to laugh when a small dirty rag doll is tossed behind him, hitting him in the back of his head before dropping to the ground.

Looking behind him, he notices the rag doll lying on the ground and picks it up when he sees the words "run, run away" written on it very small script in black coal. Then he looks around to see where it came from. He sees a little girl looking at him, hiding behind an open door to her house. Leaving his bench, he walks toward the door. He is met by the child's father, who grabs it from his hand, looks back at his daughter, shakes his head, and says, "Thank you," and closes the door in his face slowly.

Wier quietly notices people staring at him but again saying nothing while most are in celebration and entertaining the soldiers as grand guests. Wier grabs Snourn from behind, making him choke on his drink.

"What the devil are you doing?" coughed Snourn.

"Quiet, and come with me," said Wier. "I am telling you, something foul is going on here."

"You better hope so. That was good milk I was drinking there before you made me spill it all over myself," protested Snourn. Now

Snourn was a big, burly-bearded fellow with thick arms and legs and a bald head. He looked a lot meaner then he was for he had a heart of gold. Still, he was a true warrior and was very strong. He and Wier were the best of friends.

Wier was sort of a clown who liked to make sport with everyone. He was smart but wasn't the bravest of soldiers. In fact, many of the men feel he is only among them to lighten the mood when times are trying. He has been known to have a steady bow as an archer, and when pushed, he fights with conviction, always is he there for his fellow band. Leaving their company behind unnoticed, they stroll away and walk around the town, where nothing seems out of place. On they walk, past more playing children and people with smiling faces waving at them or happily doing chores, going about their business. The roads are cobblestone or dirt, with deep grooves from carriage wheels carved in the hard dusty earth.

Turning the corner next to a drinking tavern called Split Foot, they see a crowd of villagers placing wagers and carrying on loudly in a large circle. Wier and Snourn look at one another, wondering what is going on when Snourn pushes himself through the crowd along with his friend to see a large boar in a wooden pen angrily snorting and grunting.

"What is this?" asked Snourn to a village guard standing by, watching.

"This is something we do to pass the time while testing one's mettle," said the guard.

Then two children, a boy and a girl, step up sheepishly to the door of the large wooden pen when the boar bangs against it, shaking its posts and bringing the crowd to a frenzy.

"What is the meaning of this? What are those children doing there next to the pen?" protested Wier.

"They are about to show their measure of bravery, my friends," answered the guard with a sleek grin upon his face.

"What do you mean?" asked Snourn with a look of concern.

"They are not going to let them in there with that boar, are they?" shouted Wier. "It will tear them to pieces."

Snourn and Wier try to run past the guard to stop the madness when the guard halts them both with one arm. He holds them in place with incredible strength and slowly shakes his head from side to side, saying no, leaving them stunned at the grip of this man who does not budge though they struggle to stop what is taking place.

The crowd is wild with anticipation, prodding the boar to madness with sticks and throwing rocks at it while an old gentle-looking man encourages the children to enter the pen, saying "It's okay, you can do it. You can do it, children."

The old man is balding, with curly hair, a round fat face, a large belly, and short arms and legs. He looks around quickly, grabbing the two children who were about eight years old, dressed in all white gowns and bare feet, and tosses them over the gate into the pen, where the angry boar charges at them at full speed.

Wier and Snourn cry out as the helpless children run away from the boar, climbing the wooden gate, when the boar bangs into it, making the little girl fall, assuring her doom. The beast is large, with long wiry hair and huge tusks. Its eyes are red with rage as it grabs the child's leg in its mouth, squealing, and shakes her wildly, dragging her in the mud while the boy child screams out for the little girl.

The crowd then gets silent, and all that is heard are the screams of the children and squeals of the boar when suddenly, the boy begins to scream and growl, leaping down into the pen, breathing heavily. The boar's attention turns upon him, and it charges the boy. The child runs with anger in his face and leaps on the boar's back, biting it behind its head, tearing into its flesh. Then the injured girl child, covered in blood and mud, limps over to the stunned boar, which was trying to escape the grip of the boy, and gouges its eyes out with her fingers, growling and swaying back and forth violently.

Then she wraps her little arms and feet upon the side of its broad neck and crawls underneath of the boar. It squeals in pain, flailing around. Holding on, she tears chunks of flesh from the throat of the beast until it begins to bleed out, weaken, and fall. The boy tears flesh from its upper neck as it wails loudly. Then the boar breathes its last breath, kicking the mire as it dies. Both of the children are covered in mud and blood. There is no sound save for their growling, and when they see its death, they draw away from it with bloodred eyes and teeth, glaring. Then they begin to growl at one another as if to decide to which of them the kill belongs, like predators showing dominance.

The old man claps loudly, pulls out a whistle, and blows it, snapping them out of their trance. They look in horror at the boar they killed and begin to cry. The old man gently calls them over to him and slowly pulls them out of the pen and sits them down as the crowd rejoices loudly, and currency exchanges hands. Some of those who had won congratulated the children on their victory. Others lost but were still proud of the children for their bravery.

Wier and Snourn stand silently with bulging eyes and mouths agape, not comprehending what they just seen.

The guard, still holding them back, slowly lets go and, turning in front of them, says, "Are you all right? You don't so look well," with stern, piercing eyes and a half smirk upon his face.

The crowd disperses as the bloodstained children run up to their mother and father, who proudly embrace them in celebration for their rite of passage. The children look and act like all small children, as if nothing at all had happened to them.

Then Snourn and Wier gather their composure and, saying nothing, nod at the guard, who nods back and walks away from them. Out of nowhere, some of those families with somber faces begin to creep forth and slowly enter the pen and, with a rope, haul away the boar to be dismembered and readied for consumption.

The two men of Chidarra follow them and, looking around, see deep claw marks and gouges in the doors of many of the homes. The tavern called Split Foot is rowdy and full, even in the morning, with drunkards and women of ill repute while shops open and customers come and go as in any other town.

As they continue to walk in a daze from what they had seen, they notice that the cheerful faces and greetings they were met with before have lessened and been replaced by glaring stares and looks of suspicion.

Looking around, they notice the high wooden walls with iron spikes and glass shooting inward instead of outward, with men in wooden lookout posts atop the gates staring at them, saying nothing. They also notice a teenage girl of definite privilege wearing a white shawl. She is alone, being greatly avoided, as if feared by others, and ominously following them. Then they hear a call from behind.

"Where have you two been? The captain has been looking for you," asked a fellow soldier.

Wier and Snourn look at one another, then Snourn asks, "Are we leaving soon?"

Surprised, the soldier responds, "Yes, that's why we were sent to find you. The captain wants us packed and ready to go in a few hours. Provisions are made by our hosts, Master Blaeld and his lady, Emwet. Is something wrong? You look troubled."

Wier and Snourn look at one another, and Snourn says, "You have no idea. The farther, the better."

Shaking their heads, they hurry back. They find Luic a bit unsettled by their absence.

The food, along with the spread of tables and benches, are all gone, save for two that are being cleared and put away by the servants.

"Where have you been?" asked Endrr. "The others are getting ready to depart. Never mind. Just hurry to prepare your things so we can leave within the hour, and that's an order," said Endrr.

Later, after the two friends clean themselves and are drying off in the bath huts, Endrr approaches them while they are covered in their towels. Both of them stand at attention until he bade them to be at ease and says, "What were you doing walking about the town?"

"Uh, nothing, sir. Just taking a stroll about," responded Snourn evasively.

Then Endrr walks over to Wier as he is putting his shirt on, looking sheepishly, and asks him, "Are you sure?"

Then Wier cannot contain himself and says, "This place is evil, sir, most foul indeed, and we can't wait to be rid of it," whispered Wier as a few villagers pass by the hut.

"You mean the fact that the gates have barbs pointing inward instead of outward for incoming foes? Or could it be the somber faces of some whilst others embrace us with friendly hospitality, too friendly, some may say? Perhaps those smiling faces seem to belie a hidden agenda of some sort?" asked Endrr, leaning on a post and handing Snourn his shirt with a half smirk.

"Oh, thank God, sir, we thought no one else knew that something was wrong here. Wier is the one who first made it known to me that something was dark, but neither of us could have imagined what we saw, sir," said Snourn, shaking his head in terror and disbelief.

"What? What did you see?" asked Endrr. "What has you both so shaken?"

After they tell Endrr what they saw, he tells them to say not a word of it, that he would make Luic aware something was afoot privately. Moreover, he would remind him of how Nuntis was uneasy and how he would not eat or drink anything. Luic would no longer be able to ignore it. Then Wier remembered and told Endrr of what he had seen last night outside and of the little girl with the doll.

After hearing this, Endrr commanded Wier and Snourn to act as if nothing was wrong, and they left the bathhouse with a smile, being cordial to their hosts when they walked past them in the streets. Endrr looks up and sees soldiers looking at them from the rooftops and waves at them, but they do not respond. The gravel roadway kicks up dust as they walk faster, watching closely the people of Turnskin. Finally, they reach their sleeping quarters. There they see the men all but ready in the street, with their horses awaiting them, packed and ready to go speedily.

"I see you have our horses and belongings packed for us already. Now that's service," said Wier, smiling nervously.

"Well, I guess that's it, sir," said Snourn. "We can go now."

Luic listens to Endrr's words intently, then commands the men to mount their horses. Slowly, the Chidarran soldiers make their way to the castle, where they are met by Rothiro, Blaeld, and Emwet, along with many villagers, soldiers, and village elders. Some wave at them while others stare. Still there are those hopeless faces mingled among the crowd.

This does not go unnoticed by the warriors, but they hold their peace. Wier looks around, wanting to get as far away from this place as he can and none the faster either. It is then that he notices the little girl standing next to her father holding the doll in her hands. Her father holds her close, trying to be seen and yet not be seen by him. For they stand slightly behind a tree, with its leaves obstructing the soldiers' view but just enough to still be seen. Wier makes eye contact, seeing the blank face of the child and her farther. Then carefully he nods at them quickly before turning his attention to the Turnskin elders.

"It truly was a pleasure meeting you and your men, Luic. We hope that your provisions were acceptable, and we wish you well on your journey to your kingdom, although you are perfectly welcome to stay as long you like," said Blaeld.

"No, we would not trouble you or your people any more than we already have Lord Blaeld, for you have done quite enough already," responded the captain. "We are truly grateful for your hospitality, but we must be off for time runs short," said Luic.

Luic notices Nuntis's red eyes glare, the hair on the wolf's back standing up.

"Your wolf is impressive. I am sure he will be a good companion to you on your journey for I sense a strong spirit within him," said Emwet, smiling in a comforting manner.

"He is as one of us. Milady, forgive our rudeness, but we must be off," said Luic.

"Indeed," said Blaeld. "You picked a good day to travel for tonight is a full moon, which can guide you even further on your journey with its light. You can make up much needed time if you so choose to travel at night."

Then Blaeld tells Rothiro to take Ilimu and Vilkatas, two tall and large royal guardsmen, and escort the men to the west gate entrance so they may leave.

"May the god Limikkin guide you on your journey my friends," shouted Blaeld.

With that declaration, the village waved and cheered them off. As they slowly followed Rothiro and his two elite captains, Wier takes one more look back by the tree where the little girl and her father stood, but they were gone. His heart sank for them and all those with sad visages they are leaving behind, for he has seen enough to know that great evil lurks here that chills his blood. He shakes his head and deems to forget about this place. Leaving it and its inhabitants far behind, they stride until they reach the west gate. Rothiro commands it opened while Ilimu and Vilkatas stand with sheathed swords and stern eyes next to him.

"Take this road through to the gray valley until you reach the mountain pass of Nuris. From there, you should find your way or at least meet someone who can point you further in the right direction," said Rothiro.

"Thank you, Rothiro, and now we are off," said Luic, nodding at his host. It is then that Rothiro notices the large clubs trailing behind two of the horses on the ground by rope. His nostrils pick up the foul scent of the ogres as he looks at his men and they at him.

"Close the gates," he shouted at the gatekeepers, who shut the large black wooden gates until a bang is heard and the gate is locked. The watchmen look out from their towers sullenly as the men of Chidarra disappear behind a group of trees upon a hillside path.

It is a hot midday sun that beats upon them unrelentingly. However, the heat is not what bothers them as they travel, looking at the countryside around them—rolling hill cliffs and small mountain ranges as far as the eye can see but hardly any sign of civilization. Their minds wander to those faces; those faces of silent dread haunt them on their journey to a man, as they reach a small ridge overlooking the rough landscape below. Luic sits still upon his horse and takes a long breath with his head down in deep thought when Wier approaches on his horse with Snourn beside him.

"Forgive me, sir, but I must say something," said Wier with a trembling voice.

"I already know, my friend, your heart is troubled about those we leave behind," said Luic.

Nodding his head, Wier responds, "Their faces haunt me. I sense something very dark shall befall them if we do not go back there. What Snourn and I saw with our eyes was horrible and dreadful, and I fear the worst is yet to come. Captain, I feel if we do not go back, their blood may be on our hands. Perhaps we took this path in the fork for this very reason."

Nuntis pants, and a soldier dismounts, giving him his first drink of water since leaving the gates of Turnskin.

Luic turns his horse around and faces his men and says, "My brethren, do you not feel it in your breasts that we should go back and face whatever evil lurks in Turnskin and not to abandon the hopeless? Was it not told to us that we should fight evil and be not afraid for the Lord our God is with us?"

The men listen closely to the words of their captain, and they thirst for battle.

"Shall we go and leave them to a possible fate most dire and have their blood on our hands, or shall we at least go back and see what truly transpires in that place? If it is as we suspect, then we shall meet it head-on. If not, then we shall turn and be on our way. Either way, our suspicions shall be confirmed or denied this day," said Luic.

Then Endrr raises his sword and says, "We shall return to Turnskin stealthily and wait for night, for the darkness shall be on our side to conceal us. Hurry, men, and let us ride quickly."

It is now twilight, and the stars are beginning to sparkle in the night skies. The moon is full and bright, save for the faint cloud cover that moves in and out overhead.

Endrr sends two scouts to go unnoticed and climb the highest and closest trees to see what transpires inside the gates of Turnskin. The scouts do just that, using the cloud cover as an ally while the rest of the troops wait far behind a hillside covered with thick grass and trees. The scouts swiftly survey the situation and see a watchman on a tower looking around and then turning to face inside the gate. They use this opportunity to run as fast as they can, reaching a group of tress close to the wall, but not close to a watchtower. It is thick with leaves and branches to shade them from being seen.

From there, they look inside Turnskin, and nothing seems that unusual. Many bonfires give off much light appear as far as the eye can see. Looking around, they see many people gathering in a hurried fashion in the village square near the castle. The center is becoming a mob scene, with people shouting and scurrying about. The streets become lined with people wall to wall throughout Turnskin, with many holding torches. Even the watchmen leave their posts to join the spectacle, raising their hands and looking up in worship of the bright moon that shines its light upon the earth.

Then the people begin to shriek and howl in an unholy fashion, dancing and twirling about as if in a trance. One of the two spies tells the other to "go and send for the others because something afoul seems to be taking place."

He climbs down the tree, sends for the rest of the men, and tells them to get closer and await his fellow's signal. Luic gathers the men, and swiftly they dismount and follow, leaving their steeds behind with a few men, ready to escape if need be.

The sound and sights inside become more and more macabre as men, women, and children begin to tear off their clothes, dancing and singing to the moon above. Then an eerie low-toned bell sounds, and soldiers go only to the doors with claw marks etched deep in the wood that begin to glow red and gathers all those with hopeless faces. Now their silence is replaced with crying, and their faces are wrought with absolute terror as they are forcibly removed from their homes, kicking and scratching. The young and the old alike are tormented, none are spared, as the sound of their screams, as well as the shrieking howls and musical dance of their tormentors, is at a fever pitch.

The spy yells for the captain, and that is all that is needed. The men charge the gate, trying to look inside when the spy in the tree sees the large wooden gate locks move back on their own, and the gate opens wide with no one in sight. His eyes cannot believe what he sees. He jumps out the tree and runs to the captain, who awaits his word.

"Who opened this gate? Did you see? Are there any awaiting us?" asked Luic.

"No, sir, the gate locks open by themselves, as if by the hand of God himself. Not one is here, for all are in the streets leading to the castle. The screams you heard are those we seek, for they gathered from their homes, young and old alike," said the spy.

"The opening of the gate is a sign from the Lord that he is with us, for in truth, I feel his presence resting upon our band. Whether we face few or many, or even if we die, we shall not fear, nor shall we abandon those whom we came for. Follow after me, and may the

God of Feneer light our way," said Luic to his men. Then one by one, they swiftly follow their captain, their drawn swords glistening in the moonlight.

Running on the rooftops unseen by the crowds below who are focused on the moon, they reach the castle, where they see all the abused wailing in great fear. Then Blaeld, holding a large book of incantations, approaches with Emwet, surrounded by the elders, all wearing black robes on the balcony of the black stone castle over-looking the village. An eerie silence descends upon them. The people sway back and forth in an evil rhythmic manner, as if awaiting a climax.

Wier searches for the little girl and her father, and beside him is Snourn, searching with him, when Blaeld speaks. "People of Turnskin, those who by divine right rule amongst mankind and over those who are but ignorant fools, tonight is our night, for is not the moon full and its light bright? Are we not strong and invincible, eternal and wise? The more we feed, the more we multiply. The more we multiply, the stronger we become. The stronger we become, the weaker the race of men shall be. These cattle, the humans whom live among us, are but feed to us. For this night, some shall burn whilst others shall be turned."

Then Emwet raises her hands and orders the separation as guards pick many from the encircled terrified group and place them before the balcony when Emwet speaks. "You fortunate souls of this quiet village formally known as Sming and now walled and known as Turnskin have been chosen to become better and more than you are now. Look at yourselves. I was once as you are—weak, pathetic, and simple. After tonight, you shall be so much more, for you shall become strong, potent, and wise. Rejoice, my friends, and look about you, for you shall become one of us. You shall become immortal, as divine as the gods themselves, and you shall thirst for the flesh of men and beast alike, and you shall never be a weak, lesser vessel again. Do you hear, fools, you shall be as we are, and we shall become one."

The crowd begins to howl, dance, and shriek when Blaeld qui-ets them. Then he turns to the other group of victims and says, "You are not as fortunate as your brothers for you have not been chosen for turning, but rather for consumption. Your flesh burn and shall satiate our gullets as your blood quenches our thirst."

Then Wier spots the child and her father in the group to be devoured and points them out to Snourn.

Blaeld gives the order for the grand feast to begin when Luic cries out, "Blaeld, you shall not have the innocent this night. Nor shall they ever be tormented by you again."

"Who dares curse me and interrupt our ceremony?" screamed Blaeld in sheer shock at the tone of defiance. The crowd looks up and sees the men of Chidarra with swords raised and bows, axes and shields prepared for battle.

"We dare, the host of Chidarra and bane to destroyers such as you who lay waste to the innocent," declared the captain.

"You, it is you, Luic, those whom we fatted like lambs for the slaughter today and sent away full," said Blaeld. "The gods are with us this night, my people. For we were going to slaughter them on the way for the sport of the chase. Now have the fools come back to us to be devoured on their own accord. Fools, do you not know what takes place about you? If not, then we shall show you."

Suddenly all eyes turn upon the men on the rooftops, and a swift wind blows out all the torches and bonfires throughout the village. The glare of the moonlight is all that is needed to see what happens below them as hundreds of red eyes pierce the darkness, looking at them.

The screams of fear by the helpless victims can be heard crying out over the deep growling, and in the bright moonlight, Luic and his men could clearly see "a" grotesque scene unfolding below. Long snouts and white fangs replace the teeth of men. Long pointed ears, and a coarse, hairy mane of diverse colors sprout to cover their bodies. Larger they grow before the very eyes of the host of Chidarra, with claws that sparkle in the dark. All but those held captive change form, save for the youngest of them who become as feral as the children who slayed the boar.

Finally, Blaeld turned into the most evil creature of all, a two-horned reddish werewolf grown much larger and more terrible than the rest. Upon his neck is a gold amulet in the form of a pentagram.

His wife changed into a white she wolf, dreadful to behold, with coal black eyes, large teeth, and claws. Both they and the other elders were still robed while the rest shed their clothing completely, save a few who wore shredded attire. Then the king wolf orders his subjects to attack only Luic and his men. Thus, they race upon the rooftops to slay them with frothing maws and claws open to devour and tear apart the would-be avengers.

But the Spirit of the Lord was with them, and their aim was true. With great agility and stamina, they outmaneuvered their foes and, having the high ground, awaited the evil spawn to come to them and taste their blades. With swiftness and accuracy, their weapons cut off the heads of some while cleaving others in two. Arrows found their mark without fail while the ax hacked and sent others to their ruin. Endrr took fifteen of his fellows, leaped down from the roofs, and surrounded the prisoners, protecting them from the hellish brood. God sent a madness upon their foe and turned many of the werewolves against each other as they tore one another apart. Wier and Snourn stood in front of the father and his daughter and cut them loose from their bonds, as well as the others who were to be devoured. The battle raged, and sensing Blaeld was about to do something foul, Luic fought his way to the ground, entering the castle, where he saw beautiful paintings and sculptures that turned horrific before his eyes. Speeding up the stairs, he sneaks to a dark smoke-filled pillared room with nine thrones in a circle of sorcery. In the middle on the floor, a pentagram is etched in blood, with candles as Emwet and the elders pray to their god Limikkin for power.

When Blaeld looks upon his many fallen and the destruction of his people, he becomes enraged and breathes deep from his lungs, blowing a strong wind that scatters man and werewolf alike. Empowered by arcane prayers to Limikkin, he blows his foul breath and scatters them again, giving his minions a moments respite to gather their strength and wits about them. Again, he blows, but this time he aims at the humans and smashes them to the ground and against buildings with a poisonous vapor, giving them pause. Luic sees his chance while the elders are distracted, and as the king werewolf prepares to blow again, he throws a dagger into the back of

Blaeld, causing him to scream, blowing fire below at his own kind, burning them alive.

Enraged, Emwet lunges, along with the elders, to attack Luic, who calls on the name of the Lord. He causes them to lose their wolf forms and return to those of mankind.

"What happened? This is impossible!" screams Emwet. The shock of their transformation freezes them for the slightest instant as Luic, joined by soldiers entering the sanctuary, seize the moment, piercing them through the heart many times as their bloody corpses crash to the floor.

Feeling his powers waning, Blaeld hears the screams of a girl behind him in the occult throne room. That gives him and Luic pause. Hiding behind dark red curtains is a lovely girl child, about thirteen years old, wearing a stunning indigo gown long and sparkling. Her skin was pale white. She had red hair, beautiful hazel eyes, and bare feet wearing gold anklets, and she was shivering in the shadows, unseen by Luic when they slew Emwet and the elders.

When Blaeld saw the child shivering in terror and looking down upon the bodies of Emwet and the elders broken before him, he let out a scream that shook the foundations of the castle—nay, even the entire square below and the homes about them. Luic and his men fell off their feet due to the tremor and shaking. They held their ears when Blaeld let out a white flame from his lungs, burning the pillar that Luic hid behind as his men ran for help. Some of the werewolves fled the village after seeing the deaths of so many of their comrades as the rest fought on, but to no avail, for the host of Chidarra made a great slaughter of the wolven clan, decimating their ranks. Others, taken by the madness, slew one another as if they were fighting their darkest most hated enemy.

Endrr yells to the archers on top of the roofs to light flaming arrows and set the village ablaze. Then he gathers men from below and lights torches, burning homes and all that they can. Then he says to Snourn, "Gather the men and get the prisoners to safety, along with as many steeds in their stables to take for our journey and await us where our horses are. Wier, go with him and gather the troops.

Slay any who get in your way. I must find Luic before this place burns to the ground."

Then three soldiers call out to Endrr and say, "Sir, the captain's in danger. He faces Blaeld."

Endrr motions for them to follow with weapons ready, and with his sword in hand, Endrr runs inside the castle, where he hears the sounds of battle upstairs. "Wait here and hide yourself. Fire upon any who is not of our band in secret while I go to the aid of our captain," said Endrr.

When he reaches the summit of the stairs, he sees Blaeld battling Luic, knocking over several black stone columns, trying to summon more flame to burn him alive. However, he cannot for his power is spent. He hacks away with his claws at Luic's glistening shield, which burns his hands, causing him great pain as Luic's sword slashes his face when something catches his eye.

Noticing Endrr, Blaeld is distracted, and Luic's blade sinks deep, burning inside his chest. Luic sees the child still shivering, wrapped in the curtains, and yells for her to run. When Blaeld sees this, he can hardly muster the strength to weep as he cries out, "Noooo! Emwet, my queen and my princess! You took all I love, you human scum."

"A curse be upon you and your house as you have done to me and my house, Luic of Chidarra. May your beloved die before your eyes and your seed know exile and your household come to a burning ruin as mine has now been laid waste. I summon this curse upon thee, self-righteous one, and as a bird always finds its nest to rest, may this curse, as a fowl flies swiftly, find its nest resting upon your crown." Then the great werewolf utters dark sentences as he pours all his being into the curse that he pronounces upon Luic.

Broken and spent with one last prophecy uttered, he laughs and says, "Ha, ha, ha, I see a great war coming. Darkness against light, darkness against light. Too bad for you, o King, for by your own will as my own, your horn shall be broken of your own hand." Then he grabs his left horn and breaks it off his head.

With those last words, Blaeld the king dies, having poured the last remaining evil enchantments and malice from his dark heart into the curse upon his foe. Then Luic takes his sword, severs the head of Blaeld from off his body, and sets ablaze his palace but not before keen eyes take notice from a window in a building across the terrace, looking in to see the death of the wolf king.

An archer races upstairs and cries out, "Captain we must go. The village is set ablaze. We're all that's left, and they await us by the hillside."

"Did you see the girl, the girl in the gown?" asked Luic frantically.

The archer, looking puzzled, asks, "What girl?" as they run past and over burned dismembered bodies. It was so great a slaughter, so great a victory over a monstrous enemy that was set to plague many lands.

The fire burns in the night sky. Smoke ascends higher and higher, blinding them. Finally, they reach the west gate, leaving behind a once-proud town that had gone the way of darkness and finally to perdition. Those that escaped and are among them are about 450 men women and children. All pause to look at the burning symbol of death. That place of terror called Turnskin is no more.

The flames reach high into the night with a crackling sound of wood and stone loudly burning forth. The fire from the blaze heats and lights the night almost as if it was as the rising of the sun in the morning. Endrr stares at the flames of the burning village and the smoke that billows from it, and it is then his thoughts turn to what truly had happened that night.

"For us to have won such a battle against so many unnatural foes, the hand of the Lord was truly with us. There is no way we should be alive, a band of forty against hundreds, if not thousands," whispered Endrr.

Then Luic put his hand upon Endrr's shoulder and said, "Your thoughts are as all of ours, my friend. It was as though my arm was guided and my blade truer than it ever was before. How it pierced the flesh of the werewolves who have thick muscular hides covered with long fur and are stronger than ten men?" Pulling his blade from its sheath to look upon it, he discovers it was not fashioned of steel but was now of pure silver yet harder, sharper, and lighter than steel.

Endrr looks awestruck, pulling out his blade to discover his sword too was silver, and says, "This-this is impossible. How? When did this happen?"

Then every soldier examined his weapon, and all were silver, to their surprise. Even the archers' bows, arrows, and bowstrings had become silver. All changed form from steel and iron to the brightest, strongest, and lightest silver. Even the bows, though silver, still bent as wood as did the bowstring.

The men acknowledged the miracle and went upon one knee, silently thanking God for helping them save the innocent and slay the werewolves. It was David, the father of Lucia, the little girl with the doll that made sense of the matter to Snourn and Wier.

"May I see your sword?"

Holding the sword and showing it to his fellow villagers, they touched it, and eyes grew large with wonder. "And you say all of your weapons were made of steel before this night?"

"Aye," said Wier, "iron, steel, now silver, but why?"

"That is easy," said David, giving Wier back his sword. "It is because silver is one of the only substances on earth that can slay a werewolf. In other words, without these swords, you and your men would have surely been slaughtered or turned into the accursed creatures themselves. You didn't notice it in the heat of battle. Whatever magics or gods you serve truly are remarkable."

Then Snourn and Wier took David to their captain so he could tell him what he told to them, and Luic called his troops together apart from the villagers to inform them the reason the Lord changed their weapons into silver. Then they were all the more resolute in their thoughts toward the Lord and could not contain their emotions, crying aloud repeatedly, "The Lord, our Deliverer."

Even the villagers, who knew not God, from the oldest to the youngest joined the shouts of praise.

So great was the celebration that the former prisoners began to dance for joy. Suddenly, a hideous roar was heard coming from the burning village. From out of the smoke and flames, the form of a huge werewolf arose in the sky. It stared at them, snarling with anger. Its eyes and teeth were formed from the flames, but the soldiers were stout in the Lord and were even prepared to engage it in battle if need be, for they had no fear of its terrible presence. Letting out a long howl of defeat, it slowly lost form, dissipating into the night sky and was seen no more. Suddenly a black shadow on four legs makes its way to the company. An archer readies his bow when Luic notices that it is Nuntis, panting and looking exhausted.

Nuntis collapses upon the feet of Luic. The captain gives it water to drink, kneeling beside and petting him Then Endrr grabbed the banner of Chidarra and slammed it in the ground as a display of triumph as they left that accursed place. They marched on, finding shelter in a patch of woods by a flowing stream they called Brookwood and rested for seven days and nights.

It is there that they gather water, berries, and walnuts and hunt deer, as they were plentiful. The villagers thank the Chidarran soldiers greatly for helping them and offer their aid, wanting to earn their keep. They asked many questions about their homeland and this God who turns steel into silver like magic, He who saved them all from the wrath of Blaeld and his tyranny.

Then one of the soldiers, whose name was Illakus, was called upon to tell of the adventures they have met since being on this long quest, for he was a great teller of tales. He was denied this by Luic, who remembered the lady had strictly held them to tell none of their happenings until they reach Chidarra and word was sent to do so. This confused the villagers, who desired to thank the unknown God who freed them from bondage and death.

SIX

THE FALL OF SMING AND THE RISE OF TURNSKIN

The villagers had their own story to tell. David asked Luic if it were permissible to tell the dark tale of how Turnskin had come to be. Luic nodded yes, and all was quiet save for the crackling of the fires and the rustling of small animals in the trees and on the ground. It was sunset, and the light was dimming, making this moment all the more somber and fearful. All sat at attention in large circles with several campfires among them.

A large bonfire burned in the middle, so David walked around while speaking, making sure all could hear him clearly. And he said, "Please forgive my art of telling tales or lack thereof, as I am unaccustomed to doing so, save for telling them to my daughter Lucia from time to time so that our thoughts were anywhere but the cursed village called Turnskin. Here's our tale, blessed men of Chidarra."

David takes a deep breath and begins his tale how Turnskin was not always but was once a quiet village called Sming resting in the wilds of Haverdale, a people known for farming and not too fond of venturing outside of their surroundings. They were a proud people who worked hard, building homes, raising flocks of livestock, living off the land, and maintaining a quiet simple life.

Their community was close-knit and took pride in family friendship and a hard day's work. Nothing was better than when everyone came together at harvest to gather the crops and enjoy the fruits of their labors in merry festivals of song, dance, food, and drink. Again, they didn't seek outsiders but were known for taking in weary travelers and hearing their tales of other lands and exciting places that they have not seen.

Always hospitable and kind, they never truly needed an army for defense, for they had no enemies, only thankful journeyman that had lost their way or those who traveled long routes from one place to another. It was several years ago that a group of just such weary travelers with torn and dirty garments came to their village, seeking food and lodgings. They claimed to have come from a far-off land that had been overrun with barbarians, and they sought out a place to start anew.

They assured the village they would stay only a few days and then be on their way, and so the village delighted in helping them. As recalled, it was a group of about twenty men, women, and children, and they seemed so spent and forsaken. So preparations and lodgings were made, and they were fed to the full on meat, grains, and vegetables. The villagers took a liking to these strangers and, after a few days, said they could stay longer if they so wished.

The strangers accepted their offer and earned their way by helping out with the village chores such as farming, grazing, milling, and blacksmithing. They were hard workers and well liked, and after about a year, homes were built for them. They had become part of the community, and all seemed well. Their leader was slender and soft-spoken but seemed wise and helpful. His name was Rothiro, and he was even asked to join the village elders by Huron, their chief, so that his people would feel they had a voice in town matters and were not left out. Their wives began to bear children at a faster pace than those from Sming, and after thirteen years of intermarriage, their ranks grew considerably.

The sun had now gone down fully, and it was the dead of night. They huddled closer together as the darkness, the chill in the air, sounds of movement, and the watchful eyes of beasts in the woods played on their minds.

David stops and again takes a deep breath and shakes his head and cried out, "Oh, that we would have listened to Jeremy. Poor Jeremy." With that somber saying, he continued to tell his tale.

He walked about, saying how after a few years, odd things began to be noticed of the strangers—how they began to consume raw meat for food rather than cook it, stating it was a custom from their homeland. Also, how they seemed stronger and could do many feats that seemed impossible for ordinary men, like running as fast as a deer and tracking a scent on the hunt like the stoutest of hounds.

It was when the moon grew full and bright that the strangest things took place, for their eyes would begin to burn red as the tip of burning ore taken from the furnace. They would sway back and forth slowly, looking at the moon either by themselves or in groups, and their children at the age of six and on would start to show faint signs of oddity. They would become more aggressive to the village children and bully them, saying demeaning things, calling them weak, stupid, and inferior. The village wives or husbands that married the strangers were even becoming frightened of their spouses' behavior and sadly even their own children.

"To keep the peace, we all held silent about what was going on. We compromised and would later pay dearly for it—all that is, save for Jeremy, for he would make mention of dreams that haunted him in the night about these people as time went on."

He went to Huron and the council about it but was soundly overruled and humiliated for his accusations by them and everyone else in the village. It was strange that his only would be ally was Rothiro, who tried to calm his fears and even persuaded Huron not to banish him for what he called gross and damnable accusations. Jeremy cried all the more that something was not right with this clan and that they should be ousted from the village. He became ostracized and was labeled a disturber of the peace. His own wife and children would have nothing to do with him. That is when he cried out, saying, "Oh, my people, my people. Something has bewitched you.

And you, my beloved and beautiful, my wife, Emwet, who I adore above all else, save our four children, will you as well abandon me?"

Emwet gave no answer but looked on as if her husband had gone mad. Then holding her children tightly, she turned her head, and the order was given to banish Jeremy. So the deed was done, and Jeremy was gone. Cast out and alone, he lived in the wilderness but always did he yearn for the love of his family and the safety of his own who spurned him.

It was not long after that more strangers had come to the village and to the surprise of all, they were the kinfolk of Rothiro's clan. However, they were not clothed in rags as he and his ilk were when they first appeared. They were beautiful to look upon and stout, dressed in almost regal attire. They were well read and versed in knowledge, and their count was about two hundred men and women. They bore swords and shields and were adept in the arts of healing, philosophy, and astrology. Their leader was tall, with long black hair and eyes that almost mesmerized any he looked upon. He wore a gold amulet with a five-pointed jewel encrusted star in the middle of it, and when Rothiro saw him, he ran and bowed before him as one would a king.

"His people were welcomed as our own without question, for they were the kin of Rothiro and his people who came years before. It was exclaimed that this man was the prince of a great kingdom called Umoloth, which had fallen into the hands of barbarian hordes many years before. For years, they fought bravely to reclaim their kingdom, but to no avail, and were exiled searching for any of their kind that had escaped the destruction of their lost abode."

The sons and daughters of Umoloth were so very glad to have their reunion, for they thought their kin scattered or lost to the wilds of the earth. The women among his band were very beautiful and drew much attention from the would-be suitors of the village. It was the leader among them that drew the most enthrallment, not just from the women but also from men, who had admiration for his intellect, charm, and wisdom. However, his eye was focused keenly on one more than all the rest, for his heart was instantly smitten to the core with one look upon her.

"He made no bones about it at all. He saw her beauty and her spirit, but most of all, he read her heart as one could read the lines in a book, for she was lonely and hungered for companionship and love—not love for her only but love for her children. It was the lady Emwet, and with little courting and even less objection, they were wed within the month. Her new husband's name was Blaeld Ulrika, and he would soon be the scourge of our people."

The villagers shook their heads in shame of Emwet. Nuntis lies next to Luic by the fire, his eyes reflecting the dancing flames that reach high in the tree shrouded night.

Blaeld humbled himself before the counsel and gained their trust quickly. For when he came, he warned that barbarian hordes were lurking far south and would soon find this village and conquer it, slaughtering all who would not give in to their rule. Therefore, he suggested to the elders to fortify the village by making a fort or castle with large walls about twenty-five feet high out of sturdy wood and stone laced with black tar and pitch to protect it from the elements. This hold was to go completely around the whole village, but it was to leave plenty of open unpopulated areas inside for later construction of homes and farming.

Without hesitation, Huron gave heed to this request, and preparations were made for the erecting of Grimmfang Keep and Toralu, the wall Sming. Day and night, the people work and toil under the watchful eye of Blaeld. It did not take long to erect, for the kin of Rothiro were strong and do the work of several men with ease.

All the while, Jeremy lived alone in the wild, watching from afar the changing of his homeland and groaning on the inside for his family. He had no idea that his wife lay in the arms of another and that his children were now the sons and daughters of Blaeld.

After a time, what would be known as Toralu, wall of despair, and Grimmfang, the castle of blood and screams, were completed, and a joyous celebration took place. Watching nearby and unseen was Jeremy, beholding the marvel before him. He noticed that the barbed metal spikes to keep out invaders were pointed inward, not outward. Along with that, another thing caught his attention, for some of the manned guard posts were overlooking the inside of the village and not the outside for oncoming attackers. With all the cheers and celebration going on, his heart could no longer endure the pain of being without his family, and so Jeremy approached the gate.

Looking up at the armed guard, he requests permission to enter but was denied until a request was made to Huron, who asked Blaeld and Emwet if it was okay to allow him entrance. After much consideration, they agreed it was fine as long as he remained peaceable. Therefore, Rothiro was sent and ordered opened the gate, where he met Jeremy with a smile. The lone broken man was happy to see him, for he talked to no one for many, many months. He wore animal skins and was unshaven looking, grizzly, and unkempt. Still he was home, he said to himself.

So much had changed in such a short time to him. He was not met by friendly faces, but rather, suspicious ones. The celebration lessened at his appearance, and he felt the disdain from people who were all but his family. However, the worst was yet to come. For when he asked to see Emwet and his children, Rothiro took him to the town square, formally known as Khana and renamed Howling Court, where he saw her sitting in the lap of her new husband. His children saw him but did not approach him. This tore his heart to shreds, and so he ran and hugged them tightly. However, they were repulsed by his presence and his smell.

After sobbing greatly and begging his wife to approach him, she denied him by turning the other way. At seeing this, Jeremy ran to her and pulled her out of the lap of Blaeld. Then Huron ordered guards to seize Jeremy, but Blaeld would not allow it. Instead, he stood and called Emwet to him, and he kissed her lips and fondled her breasts in front to him for all to see. This enraged Jeremy, and he charged Blaeld, only to be met by the fists of the guards who beat him sore.

Jeremy cried out in pain of body, but more so pain of heart. Then Emwet walked over to him, knelt by his side, and acted as if to comfort him but instead spat in his face repeatedly to the cheers of the crowd and even his children. He asked why he was treated so disdainfully by his own wife when she coldly answered him. She told him she hated him and was in love with him who kissed and fondled her right to his face. Then she said he was weak and all he knew was lost forever, would never return, and that it would have been better for him if he had taken his own counsel and left these lands all together.

They were very cryptic words from one so beautiful and once so timid, for now she was cold and filled with ill malice. She had become smug since her union with Blaeld, but so have many among the village, stranger and commoner alike.

"Bewitched, I tell you. Bewitched all. Bewitched by a dark spell from the pit!" screamed Jeremy. "Look at what has become of you since they came long ago, and even worse now. Though you hated me for the nightmares that laced my pillow many a night and of my revealing them to you, labeling me a disturber of the peace, I love you still. All of you.

"Since my banishment, my constant companions were loneliness, fear, rejection, and despair that gnawed at me continually. I was without hope and on the brink of killing myself from the loss of my wife and children and for fearing for all of you. There I was one cold night in a cave shivering by a fire, wanting to sleep and never wake up when I dreamed of that mythical kingdom of peace and prosperity and their citizens, those of Itvihiland. Legend says they served the God of heaven and earth who heard the cries of His people. This seemed more than a mere dream but rather truth. Therefore, I sought the God of Itvihiland day and night in prayer and would not eat, never truly believing I would be answered.

"But one day, a peace came over me that passed all my reason and all understanding of men. My thoughts and prayers that were once aimless now had purpose. Where once I was a nonbeliever in things superstitious, I now knew deep in my soul there was a God in heaven who answers prayer. Though you hated me, He loved me and called me by name. But my heart was still broken for you, and so I prayed that your minds would be set free of the foul enchantment placed upon you oh so subtly.

"He told me what would happen to me if I came back to you and how you would reject my warnings to turn from those strangers among you. I thought I was prepared for the scorn and shunning, but I was not. Knowing the little that I do I asked for your deliverance, and he promised that one day you would be delivered but not before reaping the terrible harvest that you had sown upon yourselves. I knew then that it was better to be alone and cast out, rejected of men, but accepted of this Deity who truly lives and is no myth than to be accepted and desired by those who are headed for the doom of dooms."

Then Huron had heard enough and smote him in the face. After his assault, Jeremy bows his head, and Emwet comes over to him and kicks him in the face, and he slumped upon his back.

"Emwet, I will always love you. He told me I will soon be with my children, though I cannot see how now, for they hate me so."

Emwet stood over him with glaring dark eyes and said, "And what of me, Jeremy, what did your newfound God say of me? For I tell you a truth that shall bring you closer to death than you are now. You shall never ever have me."

A mob formed around him, kicking, biting, and striking him to the point of death.

Then with a disfigured and bloodied face and with only one eye open, Jeremy said unto her, "As you said."

With those last words, he shook terribly, looked at his children for the last time upon this earth, and died.

When David told that part of the tale, there was not a dry eye among the villagers, for they were pricked in their heart for Jeremy and what had become of him. After a few moments, David gathers himself and continues his story.

For right after the death of Jeremy, the spell that was cast upon the people for so long had been broken, and their eyes were opened. However, many in the village still clung to the new order of things and would not be swayed by the confusion running through the ranks. Huron, a few of the elders, and many of the people looked upon the dead body of Jeremy with horror and demanded that the strangers leave their village. It became apparent that he no longer ruled, nor was it their village anymore. It was now the abode of Blaeld and his accursed kin. When Huron saw what was happening, he clutched his head with both hands and went to his knees. Then one of his trusted elders took a dagger and cut his throat from behind.

There he fell and died, betrayed by one of his own as he betrayed Jeremy. Terror filled the air, and the beautiful skies became dark and gray overhead. Order was gone, and chaos ruled Sming as people ran to and fro. However, no one knew who to trust, for friend turned against friend family against family. Many households were split while others were tighter than they ever were. For secretly, many willingly turned their hearts to the great conspiracy that had begun many moons ago.

This is how it happened. When Rothiro and his people came, they feigned friendship, loyalty, and trust. However, secretly they performed witchcraft, casting spells of delusion to numb the minds of the people from the obvious. Then with crafty words and honorable deeds, they persuaded them to overlook the things that any madman could see was corrupt and foul. However, this would never have worked on those who didn't want to believe the lie in their hearts. All the blame cannot be put upon the strangers. Indeed, most of the blame rests upon those who willingly ignored the signs all around them and the warnings that they dispelled in their hearts, even from Jeremy who they chose not to believe, but banished into a lonely exile.

Year after year, the bonds of delusion became stronger until they were utterly given over to it. Blaeld sent out those of his kin to conquer villages and cities either by force or subtly. His plan was to establish werewolf covens throughout many lands near and far in secret until their ranks grew so great they could openly conquer and enslave all before them. It was said in whispers that it was his plan, but there are those greater than he of werewolves that he sought permission to execute them. From time to time, werewolves and other malevolent beings would come from unknown lands, seek audience with the wolf elders, and then leave as quickly as they came. Turnskin was not the only den of unnatural horror that plagues the race of men.

Much pain and anguish was felt that day. Sadly there would be more to come. For those no longer under the spell of Rothiro were gathered together in Howling Court and held prisoner for a meeting, as it were. Blaeld called Emwet and her children for all to see. Then she kissed them one by one and embraced them with a loving embrace as only a mother can with her children. Without warning or mercy, she stabbed each one repeatedly to the screams and horror of all who were forced to watch.

There they lay next to their father, ranging from the ages of four to nine years old. Emwet let out no tears no not one but instead walked around them on the ground, looking in disgust as though they were part of a memory she no longer had want of. Without warning, a great slaughter began, and those that were not killed became prisoners in their own homes. They were to be used as breeders and slaves for the werewolves, or they were to be turned to add to their ranks, those that weren't would be slaughtered. Some who begged to be killed rather than turned were denied death out of cruelty as a way to mock them.

Many like Emwet chose to be turned willingly without the aid of sorcerous persuasion. Emwet loved Blaeld and was bound because he promised her power and immortality, along with fulfilling her carnal, lustful desires. Never again would she be weak or know fear, for she would be strong and, as his bride, second to none in his coven. She would rule by his side. Thus, she eagerly accepted, and a ritual was performed, with her drinking blood where dark enchantments of authority were woven into her spirit from the wolf priests.

Then she undressed and was taken and lustfully ravished in an orgy ritual of black magic, where demons were summoned and entered her. Then she was bitten by Blaeld and the elders and turned on the night of full moon, where she went in a blind fury and killed two of the priests who performed the ritual. After this, she could not be bound, and she went tearing down homes and butchered several families, werewolf and human alike. She truly had become a beast of pure evil bent on cruelty and murder, for her bloodlust was unquenchable. This pleased Blaeld, for she could not be contained with so much demonic power and magic coursing through her veins. Only Blaeld dare confront her, and when he entered a home she was destroying, she even leaped upon him, but he subdued her and with a sorcerous chant calmed her, and she fell in his arms.

They later gave birth to a daughter named Velvela, and she greatly terrified them both with fear and dread. Thus the village of Sming was no more, for it became what its name implies—Turnskin. For Turnskin is another name for shape-shifter or, in this case, werewolf. From then on, all who came to the village were welcomed as if by a long lost friend, only to be tortured, turned, enslaved, or devoured.

The wolves would play their games by allowing some to escape, giving them a head start, only to hunt them down. They would welcome travelers to food and drink, so they would become drunk and fat. Then in the middle of the feast, to their horror, turn into their grizzly forms and massacre them for sport. The people would become the feast of the wolves. The gate that was made to keep danger out was made to keep the villagers in. It had become a prison and an abode of woe. When strangers did come, the humans were not allowed to say a word for fear of discovery. Not a peep was said, either to warn the visitors or to seek aid to escape. Those that made that mistake were dealt without mercy.

"For years, those few left who were there in the beginning and remembered the days before the curse clung to the words of Jeremy that the God with no name, the God of Itvihiland, would one day free the land from the terror that walks. As sad as it was, the one who was rejected and put to death first after interceding for us was our martyr. It would be his dying words that would be our only source of hope and light in the blackness for years to come.

"It is fitting that a moment of silence and reverence be observed for he that was slain petitioning not in vain for our freedom we enjoy this day and for our loved ones and those many travelers who, without warning, wandered in Turnskin to their deaths at the hands of the werewolves."

The solemn moment of silence was observed long in the night, with many sobs and tears and, after, an offer of thanks to the soldiers of Chidarra for risking their lives for them against impossible odds. Unable to contain his emotions, Luic stood and sang a short poem while all listened closely and quietly, none among them knowing that the God of Itvihiland and the God of Feneer are the same. Here are his words.

"Oh, Lord of heaven, faithful and just, who but You amongst the gods should we trust? Your kindness is without match and Your mercy without end, come near to us and never leave us again. You guided our arms so we would not fear nor shiver. You even turned our blades from steel to the most radiant silver to destroy the werewolves from off the earth in a moonlit night, setting their captives free from their merciless evil might. You and you alone are God."

With those touching words calming all who heard them, their eyelids became heavy, and a deep sleep came upon them. They rested until midmorning and then broke camp, restarting their journey to the kingdom of Chidarra. Those who were set free from tyranny were happy to be alive and know freedom, for they were excited to explore a far-off new and friendly land. Still they had questions about this God and the experiences the men dare not share

However, they noticed that some of the soldiers seemed lost in deep thought that they would not speak of. Their minds drifted to the earthen paradise they had left and longed to return, as well, as Chidarra, as they noticed some of the children walking alongside of the horses, playing and dancing and running around in the grass.

They think thoughts of the Ciqala and what befalls them on their quest, a quest to aid the mighty prophet who seemed as if he needed no aid. Silently and inwardly, petitions of protection and favor go up to heaven from some of them to God for those who they hope to meet again in their homeland. Still it does not go unnoticed how happy and overjoyed the villagers are to be free from years of terror, slavery, and death at the hands of the werewolves.

Noticing the distracted looks upon the faces of the soldiers, a woman named Quinta, holding her young daughter in her arms, looks into the eyes of Snourn and wonders. A cool breeze flows through her long brown hair, causing it to flutter about elegantly with a natural beauty. The tall, lush, and green grassy landscape sways back and forth with a low whistle as the wind passes through the thick blades.

Then Quinta, walking beside Snourn, cannot refrain her questioning as she notices him looking quietly with a somber face as if he was in another place and asks, "Are you okay, sir? Your face looks troubled, and the quietness in your steps tells of thoughts most ill. Forgive my intrusion?"

Snourn smiles and looks at the fair lady walking next to him as he holds the reins of his horse. Then he nods his head and says, "Milady, I have seen things that are so beautiful and unbelievable that you would hardly believe it, things that the mind cannot fathom, nor could the heart of men contain. It is among these things that my mind stays upon."

Quinta smiles, wondering what those things could be. When she nods, Snourn continues.

"I think of comrades we have recently met and are most fond of. Our hopes and prayers are with them, but ask me no more of it, as I cannot tell."

Quinta nods her head and smiles at Snourn, putting the child in his arms.

Shocked, Snourn looks as he sees her run off the path and into the foliage, where she saw wild roses and honeysuckle in the distance. With her heart racing, she picked off the flowers, tore a piece of her garment, and wrapped them in the hem as Snourn watched along with Wier, looking from behind giggling.

Then she ran back and lightly kneeled herself before Snourn and gave him the flowers and said, "With all that you and your band have done for us, this is the least I can do for you. May these flowers bring joy to your heart and a smile to your face for all you have been through. And you need not worry, milord, for I will ask no further of your journeys or of the things you keep close to your heart."

Snourn chokes up and quietly says thank you and accepts the gift from Quinta. Then he takes supplies from off of the horse and sits her softly upon it with her child.

Her daughter smiles and looks at the landscape as Quinta takes a deep breath of fresh air, admiring Snourn.

Snourn carries the supplies across his back as his other hand holds the flowers. He smells them as he admires the scenery, the wild horses roaming the range.

Endrr slightly nudges his horse closer to Luic's and whispers to him, "I don't know if you gathered this, but we're lost, old friend," smirking and winking at Luic.

Luic tilts his head, looking back at the long line of people and horses behind them and says, "It is one thing for us to be lost, but now we have women and children to look after, but I feel that the Lord will guide us as He did through all those dangers thus far."

"True," said Endrr, "so far the words of His servant are proving true. I mean, she did say we would aid the meek and be the Lord's hammer against evil or something like that, right? So far, I'd say there is little room for doubt."

A young lad runs up to Luic, holding a stick and pretends to play sword fighting with him. Luic smiles, making funny faces, causing him to laugh when he turns to Endrr and says, "He helped us save these people from werewolves, defeat ogres, a monster goddess, and we survived. How could we not trust Him to guide us home? And if not, great shame be on us for our unbelief."

EPILOGUE

Riding upon the deer of Avalla, the three Ciqala pass through unknown towns and villages with peoples of different languages and strange customs. Days pass as they searched for Feneer, who the mistress said was in need of aid. To a lesser degree, their thoughts turn to the destruction of their village and the families and friends they lost to the cavernous ogres. When the sadness hits them, they turn their minds to the quest at hand, to Feneer, who comforted them in their distress, and to the friends and paradise they left behind for this encourages them.

Most of all, what lifts their hearts is remembering the God who delivered them time and again and who told them he loved them not just by word but also by deed, for they greatly desired to know more of Him and His ways.

At times, they wonder among themselves if they are in a vast dream that they can't awake from. Then they look at the great mythical deer they stride upon and the fruit from the garden of delights they carry in their sacks and realize it is no dream at all. Rather, they were on a journey so real, an adventure so unexpected, full of wonder and terror that they know within themselves they were chosen to be a part of something much bigger than they can imagine or hope to understand. And though they tremble at such thoughts, their hearts are filled with faith and a sense of purpose that drives them on farther and farther into the wilds of the earth and to the vast unknown.

ABOUT THE AUTHOR

Keith Perrin is a Christian author who since early childhood was fascinated by superheroes, animation, and sci-fi and fantasy novels and movies. Keith also had an active imagination, always daydreaming of fantastic stories and adventures. His favorite book by far is the Bible and its awesome stories about this God who he couldn't see but knew in his heart and never doubted was real. In fact, it is his mother who he credits for reading him those very stories that led him to faith in Jesus Christ. Keith's desire is to write fiction with biblical truths to communicate the love, power, and faithfulness of God in an exciting, fresh, thought-provoking way but also to expose the reality of evil and its dangers, temptations, and sufferings and those invisible forces that have plagued the world since the beginning of time. His wish is to entertain while inspiring the reader's faith and to hopefully spark those with searching hearts to come to know and trust in Christ as Lord and savior.

E-mail Keith at Keithperrin7@gmail.com

CPSIA information can be obtained
at www.ICGtesting.com
Printed in the USA
BVHW030103270419
546709BV00001B/7/P